MW01119293

THE FALL

THE FALL

TALES FROM THE APOCALYPSE

EDITED BY MATT SINCLAIR

The Fall: Tales from the Apocalypse
Copyright © 2012 by Elephant's Bookshelf Press, LLC

All rights reserved.
Printed in the United States of America.

ISBN-13: 978-0-9852023-3-0

TABLE OF CONTENTS

INTRODUCTION

Disturbing.

That's the word I'd use to describe the end of the world. Should it come to pass during my lifetime, I'm confident I would be disturbed by the disruption of all that I knew. I would be disturbed that the future seemed less foreseeable. And I would be downright chaffed if the world ended and Elephant's Bookshelf Press only produced two books!

Still it makes me wonder, if the end seemed imminent, would you be more frightened of dying or surviving? Would you fear the life and death decisions you would inevitably have to face? What if those you cared about were too injured to continue on? Would you fear zombies? Are you afraid of what would happen if God had an iPhone? We'll get to that later...

Welcome to *The Fall*, the second in our seasonal anthology series. As you may have guessed by now, this collection focuses on the double-edged end of society as we know and (mostly) understand it, and the beginning of a time of great uncertainty. Some might say we're already living in that time, but then we always have been, haven't we?

For me, the appeal of apocalyptic tales is that humanity has always wondered what the end of the world might look like. In this collection, thirteen authors (it just worked out that way, I swear!) offer a glimpse of various world-end scenarios. While readers of *Spring Fevers* will be pleased to find several of its authors have returned, we have some newcomers I believe you'll be delighted to discover in *The Fall*.

We start with "Trust," R.C. Lewis's wonderful story of a family near the epicenter of the destruction of government. Amy Trueblood's "Emanate" is a young adult story that also tackles trust issues, but places them in a much different light. During the summer of 2012, you couldn't swing a dead cat without hitting a zombie apocalypse story, and we are pleased to present a tale that includes both: cats and zombies.

Of course, not everything about the apocalypse will be upsetting. (I mean, will anyone truly be saddened by the end of reality-show starlet paparazzi photos?) So we were happy to sprinkle some mirth and merriment along the path to Armageddon.

But the apocalypse is not merely a Western hemisphere concept. We close *The Fall* with an exquisitely crafted and intense story from South African author Judy Croome. Indeed, her story was so vivid and, well, *disturbing*, that I knew right away that it was the perfect way to say "The End." That struck me as an important decision for a collection of apocalyptic tales.

If you enjoyed these stories, please let us know. Send me an email at matt@elephantsbookshelfpress.com. I'd love to know what you think about *The Fall* and even what you'd like to see in *Summer Burn*—scheduled for June 2013. That is, if the world hasn't ended before then.

—Matt Sinclair

TRUST

R.C. Lewis

DAY NINE

HOW MANY TIMES HAD I heard it growing up? "Those boys in government know what they're doing. They'll work it out."

Gram trusted the government all the way to six feet under. It was sweet in a way and unbelievable in another, kind of like my kid sister Fern believing in the tooth fairy until she was twelve. At least when Gram left me the house, the government didn't screw that up.

As I scramble some eggs for Fern, I wonder what Gram would have said about this morning's news report.

"It seems the final week of the legislative session has been cancelled," says the plasticized news anchor. One too many cosmetic procedures. "Most of our inquiries went unanswered, but one source stated that since all critical issues have been addressed, carrying out the final week would have been a waste of time and resources."

I grunt at the frying pan as I hear Gram's voice in my head. *They work so hard, they deserve a little extra vacation.* My own response is very different. Since when does being wasteful stop anyone in government? Always spending money where we don't need it. Gram learned that the hard way.

"Mari, will you be home after school?" Fern asks.

"Yeah, I'm taking the day off. Why?"

"I have a test in biochem at the end of the week. Can you help me study?"

"Sure." I set a plate of eggs and toast in front of her. "Eat up. You've got that field trip today."

The news anchor's chirpy voice annoys me, so I flick off the television. A passable imitation of thunder warns us that my younger brother—can't call him "little" anymore—is on his way downstairs.

"Hawthorne, don't you ever do anything quietly?" says Fern.

"Why should I, Ferny? You're not hungover, are you?"

She slugs his arm as he passes her, which only makes him laugh. "Very funny."

He reaches over my head to get his protein bars from the cupboard, and I can't resist jabbing him in the ribs. "Sometimes I think Fern is the twenty-year-old and *you're* fifteen."

As usual, he takes it in stride, smiling and kissing my cheek. "We can't all be as mature as you, sis. C'mon, Ferny, if you want a ride to school, we leave now."

The two of them head out to Hawthorne's truck—his baby—and I quickly wash the dishes. Curiosity wins, and I turn the television back on.

"In other news on this Monday morning, peace talks continue amid growing concerns that—"

Click.

Then again, no news is good news.

Day Eight

Fern's field trip to the university was cancelled yesterday. The professor they were supposed to meet had called in sick. Maybe he decided to play hooky with the legislators.

No more hooky for me, so I head into work. The latest vinyl revival keeps the music store my mother started in business, but I don't trust my spacey assistant manager to run it alone for more than one day at a time.

Sure enough, all the blues albums are out of order, and the computers in the digital exclusives section need to be rebooted. I set to work and tell myself it's nice to feel needed.

The best part of working in the store is talking to customers, and there's a distinct trend in conversations.

"Went all the way into the city yesterday to meet with an architect, and she rescheduled on me."

"We have tickets to that charity fundraiser tomorrow, and we just got an email saying the main benefactor won't be attending. Meeting him was the main reason we wanted to go!"

"My sister has been getting treatment from the top cancer specialist for months, but today it was some intern. For the size of those bills, I'd expect more than a lousy intern."

Seems politicians and university professors aren't the only ones playing hooky.

Late in the afternoon, my favorite customer wanders in.

"Hey, Marigold, you have anything new for me?"

"Well, there's this," I tease, pulling him close for a kiss. The scent of soap and vinegar wraps around me. He must have been polishing the chrome on his motorcycle. "But I guess that's not new. That whole case came in last week."

Lee starts flipping through the records while I admire his long lines and the way he squints as he contemplates neo-punk versus retro-thrash.

"I didn't think I'd be seeing you today."

He glances over and quirks a grin. "You know me—can't stay away for long."

"Have you heard the talk? A lot of people not showing up to work. Feels weird."

Setting the neo-punk album aside, Lee gets serious. "Yeah, I've heard. Something's definitely going on."

"How bad?"

"Hard to say. We'll know when we know." Seeing my agitation, he walks over and holds me close. "You just worry about taking care of Fern and Hawthorne, and call me if you need anything, right?"

I nod. Take care of the kids—if there's one thing I know I can do, it's that.

DAY FIVE

There have been leaks.

Like everything on the Internet, the rumors started small: just whispers. I only saw them because Lee sent me the link. Now everyone's heard, but only a few take them seriously.

A lot of the usual conspiracy nonsense, but the common threads are undeniable. Rumors that the higher-ups in various fields have disappeared to special bunkers. The Coalition is through with peace talks. They perfected a new weapon, set to launch soon, and when our government realized they wouldn't be able to stop it, they made preparations.

Preparations for themselves. Not for us.

If the rumors are true.

The major news networks are all suffering the same technical glitch, and the local news teams anxiously act as if everything's normal. Their eyes tell the story of people who know something's wrong but also know they aren't important enough to be told.

I know the feeling.

Half of Fern's class didn't show up to school yesterday, so I keep her home today. The music store stays closed, and Hawthorne doesn't go to work, either. He hasn't teased Fern in two days.

I don't call Lee. Gram taught us to always keep the cellar stocked with food in case of bad storms or earthquakes. We'll be okay. We don't need anything. And Lee has his own responsibilities to worry about.

Day Four

The television goes dark, except for old sitcom reruns and a few nutjobs broadcasting from their basements. Too much free time and too little information leads to rioting in the cities, with the panic seeping out here to the outskirts. Hawthorne and his friend Reggie remind the neighbors what crack shots they are, so no one comes near our house. Reggie lives in an apartment with nothing worth protecting, so he's staying here.

It's worse in the city, which I only know because the Internet is still full of news. The public took away the government's Internet kill-switch years ago. Otherwise, we'd be in the dark as we wait for… whatever's coming.

I write up my own biochem test for Fern to take, just to pass the time.

"You're kidding," she says when I set it in front of her. "The world is ending, and you want me to do schoolwork?"

"Do you have anything better to do? And don't say that. We're still not sure what's really happening."

Hawthorne snorts from the corner where he and Reggie are cleaning their rifles. Never thought I'd be glad for guns in the house. "Right, Mari, everything's going to go back to normal in a week or two. Even if it's a false alarm, they left us out here."

"Most of the people in my building say they're running for it, going to try to get out of the country," Reggie says. "What do you guys think?"

I take out my phone and pull up the most reliable sites— the ones Lee told me about.

"Staying put is better," I conclude. "We have what we need, and all the people running are just hurting each other— gridlock on major highways with all the accidents, and some guy got killed for a tiny two-man boat."

Hawthorne gives me a look, but he knows what I'm not saying. If the threat is bad enough for the government to initiate a doomsday-bunker plan, we'd never get far enough to make any difference. Too far from any safe borders. Better to stay together in Gram's house.

A fresh story shows up at the top of the page I'm browsing. A recorded message from the president has been released, so I open it.

He apologizes.

Then he confirms everything. The bunkers, the weapon… the fact that we've all been left behind.

My brother and Reggie head up to the roof with their rifles, and I turn on some music to drown out the screams erupting through the neighborhood.

Day Two

The street is quiet again. Most of our neighbors have run, and the few who haven't are hunkered in their homes, waiting for the end.

I should feel despair, but I don't. Take care of the kids. Keep them going. That's what I can do.

Lee came over last night, briefly. He agreed about staying put and told me not to give up. Just because our leaders packed it in doesn't mean there isn't any hope. They don't know everything—I've seen proof of that all my life. If Lee doesn't give up, I won't either.

The best online source has new information—the suspected locations of several bunkers. One of them catches my eye.

"Hawthorne, I need to borrow your truck."

I don't wait for an answer and take his keys from the hook, but he moves quickly to block the door. A few years ago, I could have brushed him aside, but now he's got six inches and seventy pounds of muscle on me.

"Have you lost it, Mari? You can't go out there alone."

"I'll be fine."

"I won't—Lee will kill me."

"It won't take long. I just need to check something. Please, you and Reggie watch the house and Fern."

He stands his ground. I break out the look that says I'm older and he doesn't get to boss me around. Finally, he steps aside.

"Only because it's quiet out right now. Hurry back, and don't you dare get hurt."

I don't say goodbye—seems like it'd be bad luck.

The deserted roads make for an easy drive, if more than a little eerie. Windows are smashed on several houses, and the remains of a bonfire smolder in the middle of a parking lot. No people anywhere, but I drive too fast to really check, heading straight up to Sycamore Peak. From there, I can see for miles. I look toward the western horizon. There it is, right where the website said, in the middle of nowhere. Right at the site of the old military outpost they're supposed to be renovating. Too far for me to see clearly, but something doesn't look quite right.

No problem. Hawthorne keeps a pair of high-powered binoculars in the truck. They'd been a gift from Gram for his hunting trips.

A concrete structure, low to the ground, surrounded by barbed wire and some kind of turrets. The turrets are new. I can just make out artillery built into them. It's hard to tell for sure, but the structure is too small to house much. It must be the access point, leading deep underground to the bunker itself.

Yeah, renovations.

Movement to the south catches my eye, and I refocus the binoculars. Groups of citizens, mostly on foot, approach the bunker. Some have tools and work on cutting through the fencing. I watch half a dozen try to breach the perimeter. They're quickly gunned down by the automated defenses. Every one of them, even those still outside the fence.

No one from the outside is getting in. Only the elite, and the verdict's been handed down. We're just not special enough.

DAY ONE

I didn't tell Fern or Hawthorne what I saw, but I sent a text to Lee. He told me to sit tight. He'd picked up new rumors; he called them confusing, but he'll tell me if he finds out more. I slept in Fern's room that night.

A new leak shows up in the morning, the same information from multiple sources, several of them foreign.

The attack will launch at six in the morning... tomorrow. By six-fifteen, everyone who's been left to die will be dead.

"How can they do this to us?" Fern screams. "Why didn't the government stop them months ago, years ago, if they knew something like this could happen?"

Hawthorne and Reggie just swear a lot. Their hands shake.

I can't cry or scream or swear. I'm the big sister, the strong one.

"What do you think Gram would say now?" I whisper.

That achieves the impossible. Fern laughs through her tears, and even Hawthorne smiles.

"Gram... Gram would say the government has always taken care of us, so they must have a plan we don't know about," Fern says. "We just have to trust them to come through."

They've taken care of us, all right. Just like they took care of Gram... all the way to six feet under.

DAY ZERO

What do you do when you know you're going to die? Say goodbye to the people you love? They're all with me, except for Lee. I insisted he stay with his family. He was reluctant, but told me he loves me no matter what.

What else? Think of all the things I didn't have a chance to do? Never got married, never had kids of my own—I'm only twenty-four. But I had Lee, and I practically raised Fern, with Gram's help. Other than that, never climbed Everest, never ran a marathon, never dared try that poison pufferfish they have at Asian restaurants.

So what?

Maybe I should curse God and Fate. Rant and rave, destroy things, but that wouldn't change anything. Sure wouldn't make me feel better.

So we eat ice cream for dinner and play our favorite games. Hawthorne even mocks Fern when he wins two rounds in a row. We make it the best night ever so we can go out on top, and we fall asleep sprawled around the family room.

I'm with my family—even Reggie counts. My last moments could be worse.

* * *

Five-fifty-seven.

Fifty-eight.

Fifty-nine.

Six o'clock.

Whatever it is, it's launched. I let the others sleep. It's better that way.

Six-ten.

I kiss my brother's and sister's foreheads, lightly enough not to wake them.

Six-fifteen.

I close my eyes.

Six-sixteen.

Six-seventeen.

Six-thirty.

The others wake up, confused. I tell them to eat breakfast, and I try to message Lee. The phone's not working.

Seven o'clock.

Out the window, a trail of smoke dissipates in the western sky. Hawthorne sees it, too. His eyes are confused, still scared.

"I'm going up to The Peak," I tell him. "See if I can find out anything. Watch the house and Fern."

He squeezes my arm. "Be careful, Marigold. Come back quick."

Hawthorne won't be happy if he finds out how hard I pushed his truck up the mountain. But he wanted me to hurry, and I have to get a better view.

It doesn't take the binoculars to see. Black smoke rises from the bunker compound. I look at higher magnification anyway. There's a crater where the compound used to be, smoke and flame obscuring most of it. Nothing but the rubble of one turret is discernable.

Another vehicle drives up behind me, but I don't turn. I know the sound of that engine. When footsteps approach, I hand the binoculars to Lee.

"Hawthorne tell you I came up here?"

"Yeah." He looks through the binoculars. "Completely smashed. Did you feel the tremor this morning?"

"No, I don't think so."

"Looks like the explosion came from inside. See how the rubble spreads outward? No way they survived that."

I check my phone. It finally gets a signal up here. Forget rumors—photos and video dominate the Internet. Dozens of bunker sites are in ruins, most looking even worse than what we see on the horizon.

The phone goes back in my pocket. "Made themselves easy targets, didn't they?"

Lee lowers the binoculars, and his lips quirk into a familiar smile.

"Fish in a barrel."

Hairline Cracks

Ryan Graudin

Now

I THOUGHT THE BITE WOULD BE the worst part: watching those
rotten, snaggle-edged teeth sink into my arm; skin splitting
apart like a KFC drumstick. I thought I would scream, like
all those melodramatic actors in late-night zombie movies—the
ones they made when the idea of an undead apocalypse was
simply an exercise in mental absurdity. When I was a kid I never
looked away from the blood that shot out like Strawberry Splash
Fruit Gusher filling.

But I don't scream. And I don't look away. I'm frozen,
watching with the same morbid fascination of my childhood as
a decomposed lumberjack gnaws away at my left wrist.

Carol bursts onto the front porch, swearing up a storm and
wielding her father's buckshot rifle. She moves like lightning.
Doesn't hesitate.

Boom. Lumberjack zombie becomes his own Fruit Gusher. Though his flavor is probably more Triple Berry Shock than anything else… all those dark, decaying colors. Old blood and guts.

I feel an arm on mine, tugging me off the porch, back into the cabin.

"Oh God! Bennett!" Carol's bangs fall straight over her eyes, a feathery, yellow curtain between us. She does nothing to wipe them away. She lets go of my arm, and her hands go back to clutching the rifle. I can't see where she's looking. But it isn't hard to guess.

My wrist is a mess—two opposing crescent moons of teeth marks. And then blood. Everywhere blood. I'm getting it all over the braided oval rug Carol's parents picked up during a summer at Cape Cod. All over their cherry hardwood floor.

"Oh God. Oh God," Carol keeps saying, over and over. She kicks the front door shut, her hiking boot slamming hard against its base. "It's okay. We're going to be okay. There's a first aid kit under the sink. In the kitchen."

But she doesn't move. I don't either. We both stare at my wrist-turned-meat. My asthma is kicking in, locking stale air into my lungs, suffocating me with panic. My head feels light: swimmy. It won't be long. I don't know how I know, but I do. I feel the virus latching to every molecule, corrupting me piece by piece.

I don't bother looking for my inhaler.

"Carol." I look over and see the barrel of her rifle. A large metal O is aimed straight between my eyes. Her left hand clutches the trigger guard. My diamond shines bright on her finger.

"Do it." I hold my wrist out as far away from her as possible.

Her trigger finger curls. I look up at the sights and all I see are bangs. Beautiful, blond, too-long bangs. I wait for the shot.

BEFORE

Carol was the smart one. The survivor. I always used to tease her about being paranoid. She was the type of girl who went out of her way to avoid walking over the subway grates in New York City's sidewalks. Every time I poked fun she wrinkled her nose, hooked her arm in mine and made some jaunty statement like, "You just wait. One day I'm going to save your life."

Turns out she was right.

When stories of the attacks first started piling up in the news, Carol was the one who suggested leaving the city. She sat Indian-style on our futon, hair knotted sloppy on her head as she listened to the frantic reporters present their stories. I could hear their panicked voices all the way from my griddle of pancakes, buzzing in my ear like high-summer mosquitoes.

"Bennett! I think you should come see this." I looked over my shoulder to see that Carol was no longer sitting but standing. The hem of her baggy gray sweatpants dipped onto the futon's cushion as she bounced. Nerves shone all over her face.

"Hm?"

"There's been another group of attacks. Last night. On 86th street."

"That's not good," I said, mostly to calm her. I was more concentrated on keeping the pancakes from falling to pieces as I flipped them. "They catch the guy?"

"I—they didn't say. We were on 86th last night. It could've been us…"

I grunted. Half of the pancake I flipped collapsed to gooey pieces, flecking wet dough everywhere.

"Bennett—I think…" Carol looked back at the television screen, mouth warped to the side as she gnawed her lips. "I want to go up to my parents' cabin this weekend."

"This weekend? But Alyssa's art show is on Saturday. You know how important it is to her that we be there."

"I know. I just. Something's not right. I'd feel better if we got away for a little bit."

The little flecks of pancake mix were starting to burn. I jammed the spatula under their blackened bellies and flicked them off the griddle. They landed like wingless flies on the granite countertop.

I wanted to argue. I wanted to tell her that a four-hour-drive to the Adirondacks was the last thing I want to do after a long Friday in the studio. Carol and her parents loved being in the mountains. Hunting, hiking, skiing... They did it all. I was a city boy, through and through. Climbing up rocks and getting burrs stuck in my socks didn't really fit into my idea of fun.

Plus there was her father. His presence was in that cabin even when he wasn't. His arctic blue eyes felt like a surgeon's scalpel, slicing me to pieces under his stare. Every time, I came up short. He never said anything to my face; he didn't have to. It was all in the way he looked at me. The way he cleared his throat and bulged his jaw every time we sat in the same room.

The cabin was full of him; his disappointment. Today, I wasn't ready for it.

"We can go next weekend." I flipped the second pancake. This time it held together; a perfect, toasted-gold oval. "I was all set to repaint the bedroom on Sunday. Besides, we both know you'd be torturing yourself for missing the art opening."

Carol kept chewing her lip. She looked at the television screen. Its light blanched her skin—made it look like all her blood was suddenly gone—like my fiancée had suddenly become a ghost.

"No," she said slowly. "We should go now."

"Carol—"

"I'm going. With or without you." Her voice was as thick and stubborn as a mule. The way it always got when her mind was made up. There was no fighting her. Four years together had taught me that anything beyond this point in the argument was futile.

A terrible smell feathered under my nose, making me look back at the griddle. Wolf-gray smoke plumed up from my perfect pancake. I clenched my teeth, held back angry words as I shoveled the burnt breakfast onto a plate.

"Fine," I said, flicking the heat off of the stove. "We'll go. Now... crispy pancakes or Captain Crunch?"

"I'll have what you're having." Carol reached for the remote. The screen went black.

Now

I wait for the gunshot, eyes squeezed shut. Strange colors and shapes dance behind the blackness of my lids—the same way they do when a fever sets in. Only this time a day on the couch ingesting pouches of Kool-Aid and reruns of *The Simpsons* won't make me feel better. This is a fever no one has been able to break. Its only cure? A bullet to the brain pan.

All of my muscles are tight, wound up like one of those cymbal-clashing monkeys in the tiny red hats. They coil and clench waiting for the blast and then the nothingness.

The silence between us grows more awful by the second. It's not the gun I hear, but Carol's rigid, cutting breaths. I open my eyes again. She's brushed her bangs away and her eyes are on me. As bright and blue as the first time I saw her.

"You have to do it." My wrist is finally starting to hurt. The unnameable colors are still there, dancing in front of my sight. I feel myself slipping. "I'm already dead. End it."

Her arms are shaking, which means the end of the rifle is shuddering too. Its aim bounces from the bridge of my nose down to my throat. Carol's face is whiter than the day she watched the first report. I can see every freckle on her exposed cheek. The ones I woke up to so many times and counted while she slept on.

"No," she whispers.

Stubborn, stubborn Carol.

I don't have the strength, the togetherness I need to argue with her. I try to look around for something, anything I can use to end things myself. A gun, a knife, a blunt table corner... but my vision is slipping faster. Colors—both fake and real—blur together. I'm reeling inside and out.

"Get out."

At first I think I'm hearing her wrong; that my ears are falling apart as fast as everything else. But she says it again, "Go! Get out of here!"

I feel her edge around me, keeping the rifle between us as she yanks the door open. The smell of mountain air mixed with a front porch full of lumberjack zombie-rot hits me harder than a city bus.

She's sending me outside.

This wasn't the deal. We'd made a pact together, one particularly dark and terrifying night under the dimming battery of a Coleman lantern. A firm, unbreakable pinky swear of a promise. One of us gets bit, the other lodges lead between their eyes. Ends the misery of it all.

I try to remind her of this, but the words don't come out right. They're all jumbled, like Scrabble tiles scattered haywire across the floor. My throat is full of rasps and growls. I'm already starting to sound like one of them.

"Go!" Carol screams again and I feel a shove at my back. Her boot maybe. Kicking me with a force I never knew she had.

I stumble forward, over the awful goo of my attacker, onto the wide stretch of the porch.

No. This can't be happening. No. No. No.

Carol was supposed to shoot me. I was never supposed to become one of them.

My ears are still intact enough to hear the door shut and bolt at my back.

BEFORE

At first it was a vacation. On the way up we went antiquing off Highway 87: purchased a blown-glass lamp base for the apartment and a hand-knit throw for our futon. We stopped in the tiny town's supermarket at the base of the mountain and bought the nicest wine and cheese it had to offer. There were long, lazy mornings on the porch where we sipped cream-laden coffee and watched the mist retreat far into the valley below. I tried to make pancakes again. This time they didn't burn.

For two days that's what it was. A vacation.

Then, on Sunday afternoon, Carol turned on the television again.

Forty-eight hours has never seemed like a terribly long time, especially when wedged inside a weekend. But looking at the footage of the Upper East Side—desolate streets, smoking buildings, broken car windows—it felt like ages since we were last there.

The newscaster's voice was fast and shaky as she rattled the report, "Police have been struggling to set up a quarantine between 65th and 96th Streets, but it seems this virus is spreading at unprecedented speed. Experts have likened its effects to rabies. Eyewitness reports tell us that the sick individuals have been incredibly aggressive and violent, passing on their ailment through bites."

"Holy…" I didn't even get to finish my profanity as the camera panned to footage of an attack. I felt like I was back in my parents' basement watching *Night of the Living Dead* through the holes of a crocheted blanket.

"The City of New York has issued an evacuation advisory for all individuals not in the quarantine zone. If you choose to stay it is advised you remain inside your home with the doors locked." The reporter looked pale and slightly green. Like she had just rolled around in a bathtub full of damp Comet dust.

I glanced over at Carol. She was the same color. The remote hung limp at her side, her eyes glassy as she stared at the attack footage. They were already replaying it.

I couldn't look at the ungodly swarm of flesh, so I focused on their surroundings instead. I recognized the glass windows of the East Side Bistro and the newspaper stand next to it, abandoned, fluttering with papers. It was less than a block from our apartment.

"You were right." I looked back at Carol again, but she didn't seem to care. I didn't either. Losing an argument suddenly became the least of my worries.

Now

I sit on the porch for a long time after the door bolts shut. I stare at the ruined red of the lumberjack zombie's shirt. I look over the trees, staring at fall's tinged leaves, how they flame and sway in the afternoon light.

In the back of my mind I know I should be running, trying to get as much distance between myself and Carol as possible, but I don't have the energy. My wrist burns until it's all I can feel. My sight is falling apart, first all-blue then only black. Sounds hush, decibel by decibel, until there's nothing.

But my sense of smell grows sharper. Musty scents of earth and autumn and all the outdoorsy things Carol loves become overwhelming. I smell the putrid rot of the long-decayed body next to me; the faint deadness of nearby others in the air.

There's one smell that rises far above the others. Sharp and singing. Irresistible. Blood: living, salty, and throbbing through a living creature's veins.

I want it. *Need* it.

The need rushes through my body, brings new life into its limbs. I'm moving, slamming hard into things I can't see, just for the chance of getting to that tangy, red everything.

And then I'm not *me* anymore. I'm rended into two, body left writhing on the warped wood of the porch, everything else was… floating? Suddenly I'm above the cabin, watching my wiry, black-haired frame rise and begin throwing itself against the windows and doors. I can hear it too, snarling and raging. In this non-corporeal form, it seems my senses are restored.

In my early adolescence I had a bad case of insomnia, one that I promptly addressed by watching late night cable until I could no longer keep my eyes open. Usually it was just infomercials featuring men with cheap suits and slick hair, but sometimes there were shows that kept my interest. One of these was a feature on out-of-body experiences. I watched interviews of people on the edge of death, who talked about watching their own helpless forms on the operating table as the surgeons sliced away at their insides.

That's what I'm doing now. Only it's not doctors who are cutting me to pieces. My body is wild—a marionette of the disease—hurling against the sturdy wood of the cabin. The cabin's logs and door don't give, but my former body does. Bones and joints snap—the sounds sickening in the chilled autumn air.

I never believed in ghosts. Just like I never believed in zombie apocalypses. Guess I was wrong on both accounts.

The wild thing that's taken over my body is doing quick work in destroying it. My left arm is dangling like a limp rag doll's, torn from its joint. Blood, scarlet and still fresh, pours from a cut in my forehead. The hiking boots Carol bought me two Christmases ago—the ones that usually stayed far in the back of my closet—slip and slide in the brain bits of lumberjack zombie. Right hand scrabbles, clawing at the door, bringing up splinters. Trying its hardest to get to Carol.

* * *

BEFORE

After the Sunday news broadcast we went back down to the supermarket and bought as much food as we could fit in our car. Carol insisted we stop at the ammunition store, so we did. Supplies were already starting to run low, and the man at the register kept looking out the door with a twitchy expression. The radio on the shelf behind him spit out words like *casualties*, *plague*, and *quarantine*. He didn't smile back at Carol as he took her money and shoved the boxes of shotgun shells over the counter.

Days passed slow at first. We sat in front of the television, watching the world go to hell. By Wednesday New York City was considered a total loss, by Friday the quarantine spread to the mid-state. We didn't talk much. There were no more pancakes. No more lingering mornings of coffee on the porch.

Carol tried to call her parents, getting only voicemail before the cellphone service blipped out all together. I told her not to worry. Her father, an ex-Marine, was more than capable of taking care of himself.

Two weeks after that the power went out. A few days later we saw our first signs of the afflicted. We were on our way to town to buy more food and ammo. My Camry sedan was groaning and squealing its way down the mountain, pleading for me to take it back to the smoothly paved streets of the city.

At first I thought it was a deer. It leapt out of the bushes and slung itself over the hood of our car so hard the windshield cracked. But Bambi would've been a far more welcome sight than what was actually staring at us through the glass. Eyes blank and coated in white, but still moving. A face that belonged in a long-buried coffin, grimmer than the Grim Reaper. Very clearly dead.

We were frozen, stunned. It wasn't. It lunged at the windshield, putting another lengthy crack through the glass. This was enough to make me throw the car into reverse and shoot the grumbling Camry back up the mountain. The rotting creature tumbled off the hood and down the hill, unable to keep up with the horsepower of my engines.

That was the night we made the pact. We sat in front of the stone-cold, dead television screen and linked hands. Carol squeezed my fingers tight. My hand was wrapped around hers so wholly that I couldn't tell which one of us was trembling.

"We're going to run out of food soon." I looked over at the pantry. Its cupboards—once so full of wine, cheese, and canned green beans—were hollowed out. Only a few cans remained, standing at attention like Lego soldiers.

"I know." Carol frowned. "Too many pancakes."

Neither of us laughed.

"We can't stay here. Not with the food gone."

"Where can we go? If one of them was in the woods then the town is sure to be crawling."

She had a point. Plus the Camry's orange gas gauge needle was almost flat on the left side. Empty. I'd been meaning to fill it up on the last trip into town. Driving places was no longer an option.

"We can go out in the woods. Live like Bear Grins…"

"Bear Grylls," she corrected me.

"See. You know. We can forage stuff. Hunt. Do all the things you used to do in high school. Wilderness Survival 101." From here, if I squinted just right, I could see the picture on the bookshelf. It was Carol and her father, both of them grinning, holding up a dead, young buck by its antlers. It was one of the many pictures in this cabin I avoided looking at, not just because her father was in it, but because Carol was covered in the buck's blood. Baptism of her first kill. Seeing so much red on her face always made me queasy.

Carol shook her head, bangs swishing about like a bright yellow duster. "Winter is coming. Foraging will be scarce. Besides… you only have two capsules left for your inhaler…"

The Coleman lantern glared between us, but I didn't need its light to expose all of the words Carol never said. The truth, the real truth, was that I wouldn't be able to keep up. After a few miles of breaking in the soles of my hiking boots my asthma would kick in, crumpling my lungs and squeezing my throat to the size of a straw.

City boy. Through and through.

"I can set traps around the cabin. We'll wait out the winter here. Where it's warm."

It wasn't much of a plan, but none of these scenarios was my first pick.

"Bennett," Carol said, "if I get bit, you shoot me. No excuses. I don't want to turn into that..."

Our engagement ring dug into the sweating lines of my palm. I closed my eyes and thought of the night I gave it to her. At a candlelight dinner on the edges of the Hudson River. A perfect night; so far from this one.

"Promise me, Bennett. Please!" Her hands tightened, the diamond cutting hard into my skin.

I'd never even shot a gun before. I was always the one to press the noise cancellers hard into my ears and flinch when that supernova of noise shattered the mountain air around me. The idea of pulling a trigger was unnerving in itself; the thought of aiming the rifle at Carol was unbearable.

"I—I'll try." I swallowed and looked at my fiancée. The bright white of the Coleman lantern carved out the side of her face in the dark. Like a severe sculpture of a Greek goddess. She could be Athena—fierce and full of war—ready for anything.

I had the feeling I was somehow a weight, pulling her down, slimming her chances of survival. City boys weren't built for the zombie apocalypse. We weren't meant to survive off cans of pickled beets and syrupy baked beans.

"Pinky swear." She squeezed my hand harder, the diamond making a permanent indent. I tried not to wince. "You shoot me. I shoot you."

In that moment, with the pain in my palm and the granite lines of her face against the light, I was certain she wouldn't hesitate. She would point the gun at my face and pull the trigger.

Now

I can only watch my old body disassemble itself for so long. Like a model plane project in reverse, coming apart piece by gruesome piece. I find, as soon as I force myself to look away from my tragic undoing, I can pan around. Sort of like a camera in a high-budget film. There's a strange tug to my wild beast of a body, like I'm one of those HAPPY BIRTHDAY! or IT'S A BOY! helium balloons tied to my old self's wrist. Like my soul can't be completely free until the body is gone. But I still have a length of string. A range.

Turns out ghost-me can drift through walls. I go into the cabin and find Carol. She hasn't moved far. She's slumped against the door, the rifle lengthwise across her knees. Eyes, as empty and blue as the afternoon sky, stare at the Cape Cod rug; its braids forever ruined by Berry Gusher blood. Everything about her is still, except for her fingers. They're turning and twisting her ring. It wheels round and round, diamond winking at odd, lighthouse intervals.

Behind her the door shudders. Rattles and creaks. My body is on the other side, making snarls and groans I never knew it was capable of. Carol braces herself against the wood. Every throw of my zombie-self jars through her bones. Shakes her. One lunge is so hard the rifle tumbles from her knees, falls to the floor like a rock.

She has to shoot me if she wants to survive. The door bends more with every strike—each shock rattles the lock closer to useless metal and screws. The creature that was me will soon be through.

But Carol doesn't go for the gun. She's stopped turning the platinum band. The diamond is facing her and she's gazing into it. Taking in the dozens of gleaming facets, much the same way she did the night I proposed.

I watch her sitting against the door, staring at my ring. Carol, whose ex-Marine father pushed and molded her into the fiercest person I know. Carol, who won the Gold Award in Girl Scouts and killed her first buck at age thirteen. Carol, who ran marathons and trained for triathlons like it was scrapbooking. Carol, who watched and rewatched every episode of *Man vs. Wild* when she was down with the flu.

She'll be all right without me. Better without me.

Zombie-Bennett shrieks and the door splinters like a toothpick bridge dropped from three stories up.

BEFORE

The food ran out sooner than we thought, despite our careful rationing. It was like housing a ravenous ghost who only ate canned black olives and peanut butter. The morning of the last can was a somber one. Carol and I stood together around the counter, staring at the most unappetizing breakfast in the world: canned pinto beans.

"Why did you even buy these?" Carol ran a thumb over the label.

"White chicken chili," I told her. "We ate the chicken last week."

"White chili?" She laughed, but it wasn't a kind sound.

It made me flinch.

"Chickens..." The word glazed my fiancée's eyes, turned them a separate, darker shade of blue. "You know, I think the Barnwells have a coop."

"The who?"

"The Barnwells. An old retired couple. They live on the other side of the mountain. About an hour's hike, round trip. They have chickens… a goat. A garden."

"An hour's hike?" I looked out the kitchen window. It was fall, and the air was supposed to be crisp and snapping. Instead there was a thin haze over the mountain slopes, like the smoking rooms in airports. "Do you really think you should go so far out?"

We hadn't seen any more undead creatures since our failed drive into town, but that didn't make me feel any better. Plumes of smoke rose from the valley, like airy, black blood. There were gunshots too. They blasted at odd intervals, punching the eerie quiet of the woods. Even the animals were noiseless these days.

The thought of Carol traipsing through those silence-veiled woods for an entire hour was unsettling.

"I'll be fine," she said. "We don't have much of a choice really. It's that or air soufflé for dinner."

"What about the traps?"

"They were empty this morning. I'll check them on the way back." Carol set the can of pinto beans back on the counter, unopened. "Stay here. Stay inside. I'll leave the Remington with you. Fully loaded. All you have to do is pull the trigger. Just make sure you aren't pointing at me. Unless…"

She didn't need to finish. We were all about unsaid things these days. I hated how much the silence reminded me of her father. How his eyes blazed at me, over and over, from every framed picture in the cabin. Cutting me open. Exposing my insides, reminding me how I wasn't enough.

So I sat at home while Carol combed the mountains of her childhood. The Remington stayed on the coffee table, end pointed at the door. I watched streamers of smoke pluming from the valley. The fires down there seemed eternal.

She came back with a handful of vegetables: zucchini, sweet potatoes, and a half-grown pumpkin. No chickens.

"The Barnwells aren't there anymore," she said simply.

The second day she came back with more vegetables and a plump silver squirrel snapped nearly in half by her trap.

Day after day. Vegetables. Squirrels. Rabbits. A raccoon. Always Carol came back with something. She was in her element in a way I'd never completely seen before. Ferocity burned under her skin with the glow of the hunt. Like every time she went out into the wilderness a little bit of it burrowed inside her.

I began to think we might survive the winter after all.

The fifteenth day of my fiancée's scavenging I made a mistake. Carol was gone. And I went outside. Without the Remington. The air was ice-water in my lungs, begging me to stoke a fire in the hearth. Last night's embers were ashy and white, along with the bones of an unfortunate squirrel. I needed a few logs to get it started again. After two weeks of sitting around and waiting it felt good to be doing something. Helping. This world that Carol fit into so fluidly was miles beyond my skill set. Layering oils on canvases and cooking gourmet dinners were worth nothing here.

But wood. I could gather wood without getting too winded.

At first I thought the dry snaps and cracks of leaves was Carol returning. She was due back any minute and, I guess, for some stupid reason, I was beginning to feel safe in our little log cabin fortress.

Then I heard the growls.

I turned. Logs dropped from my arms like bricks. One landed hard on my toe.

He was a big, burly guy. Half of his decaying face was laced in a shrubby beard. A red flannel shirt was ripped and stained with purple oozes. Like I said before: lumberjack.

He might've been a lumberjack, but he moved like a blitzing linebacker. I wasn't fast enough.

Now

The door is bending above Carol, raining amber-grained wood that blends perfectly into her hair. The rifle is inches away on the floor. The ring is shining on her hand, swallowing the brightness of tears in her eyes.

I don't know what Carol will do anymore. I was so sure she was her father's daughter. That survival was her highest law. That she would shoot me.

It's like a nightmare, flipping through my mind frame by frame. And I'm stuck, unable to scream or move or help in any way. It's a terrible, terrible dream. And I have no way of waking up. No way of leaving. I wonder if this is what it's like for all the others… souls yanked along like a shivering Chihuahua behind their rotting bodies, forced to watch them feed.

Zombie-Bennett's hand thrusts through the jagged wood. Most of the fingernails are torn off, leaving bloody smears on the ruined doorframe. An arm wedges in. A shoulder. A head.

If I had lungs I'd be screaming at the top of them.

STOP STARING AT THE DIAMOND!

GET THE GUN!

SHOOT ME! SHOOT! SHOOT!

And the last thought. The one before the door buckles open altogether.

End it.

Her eyes snap up. Like waking out of a trance. They aim straight into me: clean and cutting, like blue lasers. The exact same shade as her father's.

The movement is so sudden, so decided, that I find myself wondering if she can actually see me. Hear me.

31

But I see no sign of it in her face or features. She's all concentration and speed, whipping down for the rifle and nestling it against her shoulder. She crouches, points the gun at Zombie-Bennett.

My mangled body is more than halfway through the door—made of so much blood and awkward limbs that I'm not even sure I would recognize myself on the street. Carol takes it all in, finger on the trigger. Diamond shining. Even her pinky is slightly curled and twitching, as if she's remembering our promise.

"I'm sorry, Bennett. I'm so sorry," she cries at my corpse.

I want to tell her it's not her fault. Nothing was. Not the zombie apocalypse. Not the burnt pancakes. Not her father's eyes. Not the worlds between us, and how we never seemed to build that bridge.

One of us had to end it.

Her finger twitches again, this time it's the one wrapped around the trigger.

Boom.

Straight through the skull. Zombie-Bennett drops like a rock.

He falls and I rise. Like someone came along with garden shears and snapped the cord between us. I'm through the roof, over the orange-flared trees, weaving with the smoke plumes. Rising, rising, rising.

HER

Carol stares at the ring. It's easier to look at than everything else around her: the misshaped pumpkin in her backpack, the still-hot gun in her hands, the rotten fiancé at her feet. The engagement ring Bennett gave her is the only beautiful thing that remains. The only reminder that she had a civilized life in the city. With art and wine and a consulting job. A life with Bennett. Bennett's sophisticated city life.

The diamond is still sparkling, when everything else around Carol is coated in stick and blood. She knows she should be sad, she should be thinking of the dinner down by the Hudson, when Bennett got on one knee and opened the box and all she saw was jewel-glow.

Instead Carol can only think about it how she was planning to give it back. After Alyssa's art show. She'd been working up the nerve for months, bracing herself for the jagged break. Jagged because she loved Bennett.

She really did. She loved his laugh and his art and his pancakes. This was why she stayed as long as she did, even when she felt the wrongness, the not-quite-click of their relationship.

She was going to give it back, before the strain of being together got too much. Before the hairline cracks grew and stretched and broke.

But then the zombies came and the break became sharper than she could ever imagine.

She loved him. She really did.

Carol drops the gun. With a hard, jam-jar twist she tugs off her engagement ring. She feels wrong wearing it. Besides, a 2-carat diamond isn't the most practical accessory for woodland survival. Unnecessary weight. All she needs is her outdoor gear, the hunting knife her father gave her for her thirteenth birthday, the Remington that's cocked and ready on the floor.

She'll be all right.

Looking directly at Bennett—the crush of his bones and the awful red—is too much. Carol blurs her vision when she kneels down and places the ring in his lifeless hand. It shines there, immortal, and she knows it will last long after these bodies turn to dust.

Time to stand straight and start moving. She has some packing to do.

THE LAST DAY OF FALL

Matt Sinclair

WITH HER FINGERS, BETH mimicked walking. Moving closer to the front of the recessed alcove at the entryway of an abandoned jewelry store, I cocked my ears once more before nodding in agreement. I pointed to the left and she returned my nod. I shrugged the bag of supplies we'd gathered over my shoulder and felt the few items shift against my back and sides. Foraging was getting more and more difficult in the open. Before stepping into the open, we each looked in opposite directions as had become our habit. I crossed in front of her and she followed at a jog. We had another block and a half to go to our shelter, but that's a long distance these days.

At the first corner, we stood back to back in the center of the intersection. Guns in hand, we each scanned the area, top to bottom, near and far, and we turned 360 degrees, slowly, in case anything happened that might catch our eye. I don't know if this was the best way to quickly assess our surroundings. It left us open to a random attack. But learning to survive was a risky work in progress.

Outside of a mouse or mole that crossed our path, we saw and heard nothing unexpected as we made our way to the alleyway next to our building, where we paused to eye our surroundings once more, backward, forward, front, back, and up. We crept down the alley with what passed for confidence. We'd been away for hours. Beth removed the key from her anklet and climbed up the brick wall to unlock the latch securing the second-story window. As her lithe body scaled the wall, a moment of softness slipped into my brain; I reflected on how I used to consider myself lucky that my girlfriend's body was so toned and athletic because of how exciting our lovemaking had been. Since the mid-November attacks on the cities and the rapid collapse of our society, however, neither of us had been in the mood for such pleasures. We loved each other enough not to risk such distractions.

I heard her close the window from the inside, where I knew she would reattach the lock on its internal latch. Then silence. She was inside the relative security of our building. Though I had yet to see anything threatening in the few blocks we stayed within, we remained watchful and vigilant.

A sound.

My head turned toward the front of the alley. I thought I saw something black. Did it flap? The rest of my body remained locked in place. The sound had been so sudden, so fast, that I was uncertain whether what I replayed in my mind was accurate. Something small striking metal? A broken twig? In the alley? The images didn't mesh with what I thought I'd seen.

Behind me I recognized the muffled steps of Beth in the hall near the street level doorway. Beth would always peek through the small peephole we'd cut into the metal door before opening it. Knowing that, I raised my hand to keep her at bay. I stood this way for a couple minutes waiting for a sound that did not repeat. When I felt I could, I leveled off my hand and walked backwards, keeping an eye on the front of the alley, glancing at the rooftops when I could. I felt the cold steel of the door at my fingertips, took one more glance around, knocked once and seeped inside as Beth opened the door. We gripped each other's hands and I allowed myself to sigh. She kissed me. True love, I mused.

I'd never been one to pay much attention to the media or politicians, but it turned out that they were right when they warned everyone about an impending attack. The cynic in me had thought it was just election-year hyperbole. After the coordinated attacks in major cities around the country and the rapid collapse of the stock markets, a sense of civility remained for nearly a week. Or maybe it was shock. Most of the leaders of our suburban hamlet never returned from the city, which was about twenty miles away. Three was no word from the mayor and all but one council member, who we assumed were lost amid the series of bombs and explosions. As it was, the lone council member left town as soon as he'd reunited with his family.

To be honest, we made a lot of assumptions about the people who left or never came back—things we didn't share with others. For Beth and me, it was a time of silence—not so much out of respect for those lost, though we certainly felt that, but because we didn't know many of the people in town. For the most part, we kept to ourselves in the few blocks surrounding the center of our town.

Right before Thanksgiving, Mr. Hopper, who owned the market on the corner, said he'd received a phone call that the supply truck would no longer be able to make its usual delivery. Most of us shook our heads and said we'd share what we had. I mean, we had to stick together, right? Later that day, several of us from the block met on the street and discussed the need for rationing water and food.

"Water is most important," one guy said. He spoke well and carried himself with authority. People listened to him. His name was Mark. The way he stood tall and looked people in the eye commanded attention and respect—and reminded me of my late father. He was clean-shaven and dark-haired. His wife stood with the self-assurance of a woman who knows she can stop traffic but is content to let it flow past. Their young children fidgeted beside her legs. They struck me as a painfully normal family that under ordinary circumstances would have made me jealous of their future. At that point, I didn't want anyone else's future.

"As long as we have water, we have hope," Mark said. "But we should always be watchful now and protect ourselves. Another attack could happen at any time."

The day after Mr. Hopper told us about the end of deliveries, I was chatting with him in his store when Mark walked in and paced through the aisles. He didn't seem to notice me as he bought things like slingshots and rubber bands and other stuff I assumed was for his children.

"I'd imagine your children are frightened by all the changes lately," Mr. Hopper said as he rang up Mark's purchase.

"My kids? They miss television, but they've been okay," Mark said. "I think my wife is more nervous than they are. The kids just want to stay at home and play. My wife thinks we should move somewhere else."

"What do you want to do?" I asked.

He didn't look at me. "I'm prepared to survive whatever life throws my way."

When I returned to our apartment, Beth was sitting at a table sorting through maps of the area, cropping some and taping them together. As I told her about the conversation in Mr. Hopper's store, she put the scissors down and listened closely to me. "He's resourceful, I'll give him that," she said. A corner of the map curled up, and she slapped it flat against the table top.

"What do you mean?"

"I just think he'll do what he needs to do to ensure his own survival. I'm not so sure whether he cares about anyone else."

"You've spoken to him?"

She laughed. "You don't remember him hitting on me back at that Halloween party?"

"That was Mark?"

"That was Mark."

When the water ran out a couple days later, Mark and his family left. Mr. Hopper's phone stopped ringing, too.

It was not quite December and Beth and I were among the last people still in the neighborhood. Though the cold weather tended to come late to our area, temperatures had started to fall into the fifties—even cooler at night. We'd all gotten kind of used to not having electricity, but the lack of heat was becoming an issue. In the street outside Mr. Hopper's store, several of us debated whether to move into one building to conserve resources. The way I saw it, it seemed safer to be unified. "Like a tribe," I said. That seemed to piss off some folks.

"One tribe?" said Mrs. Wall, a woman in her sixties who always dressed in black or gray even before the world changed. "Would that be a nomadic tribe or maybe an Indian tribe bent on savagery?"

"It would be a dozen or so people from this depleted neighborhood trying to survive in one place," Beth said. I noticed the vein in her neck pulsing as she spoke.

"Oh, you mean a commune. Now I see what this world has come to. I'm too old for free love, honey."

Aside from her cheeks flushing red, Beth remained calm, but I knew she was incensed by everything Mrs. Wall's comment implied.

Mr. Hopper perked up. "I think one building makes sense, too. United we stand, divided we fall, right? Safety in numbers. But if you choose to stay in your building, that's up to you. This is a free country, after all."

"Is it?" asked Dennis. They were the first words I'd ever heard him say. Up till then, he'd only been a face in the neighborhood—one I didn't see often. I didn't even learn his name until the day he first spoke. "We don't know much of anything yet since the phones went down."

"I'm sure they'll fix everything as soon as they're able," Mr. Hopper said.

"Who's 'they'?" Dennis asked.

"Well, the government, of course," Mrs. Wall said.

"The one that just got elected and hasn't taken office yet or the one that apparently wasn't able to stop these attacks?" Dennis said.

"What do you suggest?" I asked. The question was for Dennis as much as anyone, but I looked at Mr. Hopper.

"I think what Mr. Hopper said will work—if you choose to move into the building that would fit everyone, great," said Beth. "But you can certainly stay in your home. Either way, we need to keep each other informed as best we can. We should meet each morning right here. This can be our new town square. And if we have to change our living arrangements again in a couple days… well, we'll cross that bridge if we ever get to it."

A couple days later, Mrs. Wall didn't show up for our neighborhood meeting. With only about five people left after Mark and his family departed—followed by a few other folks— her absence was obvious. I volunteered to go to her apartment. The door was closed but unlocked, so I knocked and called to her. Pushing the door open, I found her hanging from a ceiling lamp. I'll admit, the initial sight was a shock, and I cried out and turned away. The fear lasted a moment and passed through me, leaving sadness—and maybe a sense of relief. It was like the ghosts I'd seen around the neighborhood—people I knew had left and others who hadn't returned after the attacks. They were wispy, ephemeral, and I soon learned not to fear them. I suspected Beth and the others had seen them too, though they weren't something we'd ever talked about. If anything, I hoped the ghosts would find their way out of what was becoming an empty shell of a town.

I took a deep breath and looked again at the body of Mrs. Wall. One of her shoes had fallen to the floor, but otherwise she was fully dressed in her customary dark clothing. The bare foot looked bruised and bloated, and I wondered if I should place the fallen shoe back on her.

In the kitchen I found a knife. Standing on the same chair she must have used at the end, I cut her down. "I'm sorry, Mrs. Wall," I said.

I placed her on a nearby couch and draped a blanket over her, like she was sleeping. Beside the couch was a table where I found a note: "I am not suited for life in a small tribe or a small town," she wrote. "If what I've left can help you, you're welcome to it." She signed it Emma.

In our apartment, Beth was sitting with Mr. Hopper, divvying up responsibilities. "Emma won't be helping," I said.

"Emma?" Beth asked.

"Mrs. Wall," said Mr. Hopper.

"She's dead. She left a note." I handed it to Beth. Though they didn't drop, I saw tears in her eyes.

"Dennis," she said, "can you go to Emma's apartment and see what we might be able to salvage?"

"Of course."

Beth turned to me. "We need to prepare for winter," she said. "Dennis is a carpenter."

Although I had no idea why his carpentry skills might matter, I nodded and offered a weak smile to Mr. Hopper. "I work in accounting," I said.

He smiled. "Beth volunteered you to serve as our treasurer. You and I need to talk later." He rubbed his fingers together to indicate money.

On a night in early December, a couple days after I'd heard the strange sound in the alley, I awoke from a dreamless sleep. Our room was pitch black. The only comfort came from the sound of Beth's breathing beside me. I closed my useless eyes and listened to her. A few taps of rain plunked against the pane of our bolted window. Was it the rain that had woken me? I turned to my side and draped my arm across Beth, and she pulled me closer. She smelled of sweat. I kissed the back of her head and felt the greasy dirtiness of her hair. Yet, I felt a familiar urge. If she wants to, I thought. But she remained asleep and soon I followed.

Sometime before waking, I dreamed of Emma Wall hanging from the chandelier. She wore a yellow dress. Her apartment was white with sunshine and she swung back and forth like a child at the park.

Mrs. Wall turned her head and opened her eyes. "Did you hear that?"

I jumped up from the mattress and grabbed my gun. Beth almost slapped me to keep me from saying or doing anything stupid. She shook her head. My eyes darted around the room, but in the early morning light I noticed that her gaze was fixed upon the window. It was as though she was waiting for something, or someone. As I joined her gaze toward the window, she turned away. Beads of water dripped down the glass, then movement in the background caught my eye. I gasped. This time she slapped me.

* * *

"You should have told me you saw something," she said.

"And say what?"

"That you saw something."

"But I don't know what I saw. I'm not even sure it flapped. I think it did."

"So it was a bird?"

"I have no idea."

She sighed and turned to the window, where dawn was still coming into view. "What else can flap?" she said. "A cloak perhaps? Was it large?"

"It might have been a small glimpse of something larger. But what good is it to speculate?"

I picked up the gun and prepared to clean it, as Dennis had taught me. Turned out he was more than a carpenter. He'd done a lot of hunting, too, including entire weeks spent in the woods. In the weeks since the collapse of our society and the gradual dissolution of our community, I found myself reflecting on stories of adventure and survival that my father had read to me as a boy. *Treasure Island* was my favorite. Dad loved *Tom Sawyer*. I'd not thought about those stories in years. Looking back, even when Dad died, the books in my parents' house hadn't sparked anything in me. But lately, well... it occurred to me that epic tales of survival are only told by survivors. How obvious it seemed, yet it still struck me as a revelation.

"Tell me about the sound you heard, again," Beth said.

"It's familiar somehow. I know I've heard it before, but I just can't place it. It's like it happens, then stops."

"But the sound, what's it like?"

"A high-pitched ping." I replayed it in my mind. "There might have been a little whistling before the ping."

"Like a whisper?" she said.

"No, more like a very soft breeze."

Her shoulders shook as she stretched her arms out toward me. I thought she'd been about to scream at me, but she paused before speaking again. "I'm trying to get a sense of what we're up against." Her voice was barely above a whisper, and I leaned in to hear her.

The silence in the room grew. I glanced at the window.

"A face!"

And it was gone. It was human. Of that I'm sure. Actually, it reminded me of a Neanderthal in a museum exhibit: bearded, an empty stare. Still, there was something familiar about it. But it had vanished before I'd been able to step closer.

"Where?" Beth said.

"I saw a face at the window. It was a man. But now it's gone. It just vanished." I looked out the window, my head moving in every direction repeatedly.

Beth pulled me away. "Quick glances," she said. "Like we've been doing for weeks."

We stood away from the window and caught our breath. I wanted to look again. I couldn't help but think I knew who it was, but I couldn't place the face.

"So it was a ghost?" Beth asked. "God knows there must be thousands of them around here."

"It looked real." My eyes were still on the unchanging scene outside.

"But you said it vanished."

"And I saw no sign of it when I stood by the window."

"For too long." She smirked and I smiled.

"Yes. Thanks for saving me." I pulled my stinky, greasy-haired girl close and kissed her like I hadn't in weeks.

She patted my butt. "You're not going anywhere without me."

"I couldn't imagine such a thing. But if something happened to me, Mr. Hopper and Dennis would protect you."

She chuckled. "Mr. Hopper thinks the money in his safe still matters."

I nodded. "He told you about that, too?"

"Of course. He thinks of me as the mayor of our building. He finds safety in that."

"You were a poli-sci major." I smiled.

"I'm afraid my degree is worthless too. At this point, I wish I had taken more psychology classes in college. What are we, four people in the midst of major sociological challenge? We're in a hopeless living situation…"

"Why hopeless?"

"We may as well be Robinson Crusoe. If we stay here, we'll exhaust our resources before we find any help. But the way out will leave us vulnerable on every front."

"The others made it."

"The others left. That's all we know." She glanced out the window, and then turned back to me. "Plus, no one has come back or arrived."

Dennis stopped by to give his progress report. "From the roof, Mr. Hopper and I looked out upon the visible rooftops and street areas. No signs of movement. No unexplainable sounds."

I stopped nibbling on a cracker. Mr. Hopper had started growing some veggies from old kits that had never sold, but nothing was big enough yet and wouldn't be for weeks, if not months.

Beth nodded. "Any concerns about Mr. Hopper's state of mind?"

"That's a pretty blunt question, Beth," I said.

Neither Beth nor Dennis acknowledged my comment. "From what I can tell, he's still sharp," Dennis continued.

No one said anything for a moment, and I had a feeling I was a third wheel.

"Anything else to report?" she asked.

"I recommend we move up our departure date," Dennis said.

"Who said anything about leaving?" I asked.

"We talked about it yesterday morning, Michael."

My stomach ached. I remembered the Halloween party, when Beth in her Mata Hari outfit seemed to be working the room all too easily. "'We' meaning you and me, or 'we' meaning you and Dennis?"

"You and I. Don't you recall?"

"All I remember from yesterday morning was that spooky caveman."

She winced.

"Caveman?" Dennis asked.

"Michael said he saw someone who reminded him of a Neanderthal. It was a ghost. It disappeared almost immediately."

"I saw it."

Dennis put his hand in the air. "I don't doubt you. It's just news to me. I've seen ghosts too, but I haven't seen anything during my reconnaissance efforts, not that I'm looking every moment of the day."

"Of course not," Beth said.

The silence returned and I felt nauseous. During that moment I realized that Beth had discussed things with Dennis that I was unaware of, things that might affect me and our little community.

"When are we moving?" I asked.

Beth looked at Dennis, who shrugged. "If it were up to me, I'd go tomorrow morning," he said. "There's nothing for us here."

"There's shelter," I said. "It's December. For all intents and purposes, this is winter. We should be holing up, not moving."

"But we're rooted in a fallow field." Dennis said.

"What do you mean?" I asked.

"He means we can neither survive nor flourish here," Beth said. "We're marooned. We need to get out."

"The three of us and Mr. Hopper?"

"Is anyone else still here?" Dennis asked. He turned to Beth. "I haven't seen anyone else since Mrs. Wall... left."

I raised my hand. "I volunteer to check the other buildings."

"You and Dennis will go. Mr. Hopper and I will prepare our provisions."

"There's still a couple hours of daylight," Dennis said. "Let's see what we can accomplish today."

"We'll start with Mrs. Wall's building," Dennis said. "It should be quick. Mr. Hopper can assess the apartments over his store tomorrow while you and I check the other residential building down the block. Finish in our own building. Ignore the other stores. We've gone through them so many times for salvage, we'd have noticed if anyone was living in them. Once we're back here, darkness shouldn't be quite as dangerous."

"Knock wood," I said.

Dennis and I watched carefully as we walked down the street, which I'd come to think of as our valley. It was open land in this new country, but it also left us vulnerable if anyone or anything were stalking us. We walked this street every day, but Dennis told me the other day that, as hunter knows, a game trail is well-traveled ground.

Mrs. Wall's building had the most apartments, with at least two on each of the five floors.

"It's better if we each stay on the same floor," Dennis said.

"That's fine. I think we'll get through this rather quickly. It's only ten, maybe twelve apartments."

"Knock first and identify yourself. Try the door. If it's open, go inside." He pulled his gun out and motioned that I do the same. "Be prepared."

"And if it's locked?"

"Bang on it a second time and announce that we're leaving after dawn from the intersection."

I gripped the gun in front of me like I was in some cop show. "You don't want me to break the doors down?"

He smiled. "If you really want to, knock yourself out."

We each knocked and looked around, then ascended the stairs to the next level.

"Of course," he said, as if we'd still been talking, "you don't want another situation like when you found Mrs. Wall."

I paused. "No. Not really."

As I walked into a room, I couldn't help but think of the dream from the other day. Finding someone hanging who could still talk would frighten me more than if I found another dead body.

"Michael!" Dennis cried.

I ran to the open door. "Dennis?"

I found him kneeling beside the bodies of two children, a boy about six years old and a little girl I thought must be about three.

"I think the boy is still alive," he whispered.

I knelt beside him and jostled the child. He felt stiff.

"Careful, you'll scare him."

"Are you all right?" I said to the boy. I bent my head toward his chest, but I couldn't tell if he was alive or not. The body felt cool but not frozen, which was how I imagined the touch of death to be.

"What made you think he was alive?"

"I thought I saw his eyes flicker."

He turned his attention to the other child. I couldn't remember what family lived here. I doubt that I ever knew. I was certain they were both dead, and I didn't recognize their faces. Death seems to change people over time.

Dennis snuffled. "The baby never had a chance," he said.

"I don't think the boy does either."

"We're going to leave him here?"

I stared at Dennis. "I don't think he's alive."

"Are you sure?"

"Please, prove me wrong." I stood and searched the room for a note, but there was no sign of what had happened. I wondered where the kids' parents were. Had they been abandoned or did their parents die? And if their parents died, why hadn't the children come to us for protection? Who were these kids?

I walked to the kitchen. A couple of chairs and empty food containers, and the fridge contained nothing but shelves.

I returned to the main room and found Dennis sitting beside the children. He'd been crying. "I'm sorry, Michael. I honestly thought I'd seen some sign of life."

I rested my hand on his shoulder. "It's okay. Maybe you did. But I don't think we'd have been able to save him. We should get back to checking the building for survivors. Like, where are their parents?"

He stood, stared at the children once more, made the sign of the cross, and followed me out the door.

We found some winter clothes, coats, and a few blankets in the apartments in that building, but nothing more significant. When we returned to the street, Dennis recommended we finish the rest tomorrow. "It's getting dark faster than I realized," he said. "Plus…"

I nodded. As it was, we had to carry the clothes and blankets back to our building. They were a significant find, I thought. Though we were still able to walk around in button-down shirts in December, we had no way of knowing if a cold snap might descend on the region and leave us prone to all sorts of new problems. The next day, Dennis and I did the same thing with the other buildings and found a few sundry items but nothing else of note.

December twentieth was our last night in the building. That night, Beth and I had made love for the first time since we'd come home from the Halloween party. Afterward, I couldn't sleep. Usually, I slept soundly after sex, but ideas were coursing through my mind. Mrs. Wall. The caveman I'd seen. The kids Dennis had found. Mr. Hopper's safe filled with worthless money, a relic of the past. I couldn't help but wonder why Beth had insisted on having sex. I also couldn't figure out why it had been so different. We were silent, mostly. Before the world changed, we were talkative lovers—as much laughers as lovers. But sex had become an action, not a reaction.

When Beth awoke before dawn, I said nothing.

"Have you been up long?" she asked.

I shook my head, no.

"I don't know what got into me last night. Maybe I'm just excited that we're leaving. God, I need this terrible fall to be history. It's funny, I'm looking forward to winter. I think I need to leave this place, go with a good feeling. Otherwise, it would have felt…"

I turned to her wondering what she'd say next.

"Oh, I don't know. But I'm glad we did it."

I smiled. "Me too."

The four of us met for the final time in our town square. On our backs, we each had our stuffed packs and floor mats—yoga pads Mr. Hopper never sold—along with various utensils, hunting knives, and water flasks. Over the past several days, Mr. Hopper and Beth had determined what was necessary and what should be left. We only had so much space, and we needed to carry enough water and have something to collect rainwater.

Water made me think about Mark, the guy who'd originally struck me as a natural leader for what ultimately became our motley troupe of reluctant travelers. I wondered where he and his family had gone and whether we'd find them again. Perhaps they'd only gone as far as the next city. It was about twenty miles away—much farther than we'd ventured these past several weeks.

"I just realized I haven't seen a bicycle in months," I said to the others.

"You know, when you and I were going through the buildings that was something I'd hoped to find," Dennis replied.

"This was always a car community," Mr. Hopper said.

"We'll get our exercise the old-fashioned way," Beth said. "One step at a time."

We started walking in a diamond formation, Beth at the head, Dennis at the rear. We hadn't gotten to the end of the first block when Dennis said, "Hold."

We stopped in our tracks and scanned our surroundings. For at least a minute, we were all silent. "I could have sworn I heard a sound," he said.

"What kind of sound?" Beth asked.

"Like a shot of some sort. But it didn't reverberate or ricochet."

"Meaning?" Beth asked.

"Meaning it's something small enough to land quickly or large enough to be embedded."

"Or both." Beth continued.

"But who would shoot something at us?" Mr. Hopper asked.

I turned to Beth, who looked at me. All at once, her eyes bugged, her mouth open as if she were in pain. She let out a slight gasp and fell.

"Beth!" I screamed, and went to her.

Beside me, I heard feet scuffle, and Dennis and Mr. Hopper shouted back and forth. I didn't know what they were saying. All I could do was focus on Beth. I held her limp body in my arms. Her head flopped to one side, and I struggled to hold her upright. How could ninety-eight pounds of muscle feel so heavy? I shifted my hand behind her neck to steady her head. That's when I found the dart. Although it was essentially a bar dart, it must have been flung with amazing force. The dart was embedded in the nape of her neck, a trickle of blood in its wake. "Oh God, Beth, don't leave me!"

I saw Mr. Hopper fall to the ground. "Goddammit!" he cried as he rolled like an upended turtle.

"Dennis, where are you?" I shouted.

"Michael, watch out!" His voice seemed far off.

"She's mine!" a voice cried out.

I turned and was stunned by a blunt force against my cheek. I fell back against the street.

I think I lost consciousness for a moment. When I raised my head again, Beth's body was already several feet away, being dragged legs-first by a man clothed only in a blanket-like cape. I struggled to stand and run at him. I fell but remained conscious. I watched in a daze as Beth's head bounced along the asphalt.

"Beth!" I shouted.

This time, I was able to wobble a few more feet before falling again. I cringed at the sound of running feet approaching me from behind. Dennis ran past. The attacker dropped Beth's legs and started to run, but Dennis caught up to him. I stood and moved as quickly as I could, which wasn't very fast. Mr. Hopper called out, and I turned to him.

"No, Dennis!" he said.

My whole body jolted as I heard the gunshot and the messy slap of a body landing on the empty street. The body of our attacker was on the ground. Dennis stood above him, gun pointed at the body.

"He doesn't seem to have a gun," Dennis called.

Or a head, I thought.

I reached Beth. Her body was as limp as before she was dragged along the road, only now her skin was scraped and pitted with pebbles. I caressed her. "Don't go, Beth. We need you."

Her eyes were dull and glassy, but I checked for a pulse. "No," I whispered.

"Michael, you'll want to see this," Dennis called.

I heard Mr. Hopper groan as he limped to join Dennis. "It can't be," he said.

"I'll be right back," I told Beth and placed her carefully on the street.

The body still had its head. Not only had we found my Neanderthal, I knew his name. "Is that Mark?"

"But he was one of the first to leave," Dennis said.

"I thought he was going to be our leader," Mr. Hopper added.

I found a slingshot, which seemed to have been jerry-rigged with a variety of rubber bands. "We're vulnerable," I said. "We've got to move Beth."

"Is she alive?" Mr. Hopper asked.

"I'm not leaving her on the street. There might be others waiting to attack us."

Dennis and I carried Beth to a front stoop. We were still vulnerable, but at least we had a wall behind us.

As I held her, Dennis checked for a pulse, pinched her skin, tapped her on the face.

"Michael," he said, "I'm sorry."

I said nothing as I stroked and kissed her hair.

Dennis looked at Mark's body, which we had left in the street. "We should probably bury him," he said.

"I just wish we knew why he attacked us," I replied.

"Probably to steal our food," he said.

Mr. Hopper shook his head. "No, it can't be that. He knew I'd have shared with him if he was hungry."

"Guys," I interrupted, "he didn't simply attack us. He attacked Beth." Words were catching in my throat. "He *killed* Beth!" I tasted salt on my lips and wiped my face.

"She was in the lead position," Mr. Hopper said.

"Michael's right, there might be more to it than that," Dennis said.

I stared at him. "What are you thinking?" I can only imagine how wide my eyes must have looked.

"Probably the same things you're thinking. They're not attractive—least of all to you."

"I don't get it," Mr. Hopper said.

I continued to stroke Beth's hair. For the first time, I realized how calloused my hands had become. Her hair felt like dry wheat. "I'll let you think about it," I said, though I don't know if he heard me.

Mr. Hopper walked in small circles on the street, looking in both directions and sometimes stopping at Mark's body. "Oh, no. That couldn't be," he said. "That just makes no sense. He had a family." Mr. Hopper walked off toward Beth's things, which were still on the street.

I kissed Beth's head once again. A troubling thought crossed my mind that I refused to speak: Mark wouldn't have killed her if the attack was about procreation. Could Mark actually have considered her food?

Mr. Hopper returned, his arms full. "We can go back to our building and stay the night, get going early tomorrow."

"No," Dennis said. "It's still early. We should go as we'd planned."

"But we need time to bury…" Mr. Hopper stopped.

"She wouldn't want to be left here," I said. "Winter starts tomorrow. She wanted to be out of here before the fall was through."

Mr. Hopper and Dennis shared a look.

"We go," I continued. "And we're taking Beth."

Dennis nodded. "Of course."

As we prepared to go forward, I replayed the past several days in my head. Why had Mark, the caveman, come back? Was he alone? If not, how many people were with him? What would we face as we walked into winter?

While Dennis checked Mark once again for anything of use, Mr. Hopper and I distributed Beth's things among us. We needed it all.

"Merry Christmas," I said as I handed him a water bottle. It was the first I'd thought of the holiday since the world had fallen apart.

"I decided to leave Mark's cape on him," Dennis said when he returned.

Mr. Hopper and Dennis offered uneasy smiles.

"Guys, we need to move forward and deal with what comes next," I said. "Prepare the best we can. We take Beth with us. At least get her out of town. I know it's not a rosy start, but we're making progress. We're no longer Robinson Crusoe."

Mr. Hopper smiled and nodded.

Dennis and I held Beth's body between us, like she was simply knocked out, an injured comrade. To be honest, I barely felt her weight at all—much less that of my pack. There was too much to think about, too many questions, too much uncertainty. Dennis shifted and Beth's head turned toward me, her nose bumping against my cheek. A misplaced kiss. I smiled. She can't be gone, I thought.

"Let's see what's ahead of us," I said.

Disconnect

Mindy McGinnis

THE END OF THE WORLD TOOK everyone by surprise; most of all Heaven's staff. We join the erstwhile heavenly denizens approximately two seconds post-apocalypse.

(GOD is sitting at a table center stage, thumbing through The iPhone. An ANGEL enters stage left)

ANGEL: *(running)* God! God! We need you out front!

GOD: *(doesn't look up)* Mmm? Why's that?

ANGEL: You realize the world just ended, right?

GOD: Oh? Uh… is that possible? I still have reception.

ANGEL 2: *(following ANGEL 1)* Did you find God?

ANGEL 1: Yes, but... I'm not sure I'm getting through.

ANGEL 2: (*waves hand between The Face and The iPhone*) God? Your Presence out front would be greatly appreciated right now. It appears to be Judgement Day. (*awkward pause*) That was on purpose, right?

GOD: Of course. (*shakes phone*) I just don't understand how I can still have recept—oh, never mind. There it went.

ANGEL 1: There's a slight signal delay, something to do with space-time continuum. Remember how *Skyrim* sold out before you got a copy?

GOD: (*rolls The Eyes*) Oh yes, *that*. I remember.

(*GABRIEL & MICHAEL enter stage left*)

GABRIEL: Did you guys not get the message?

MICHAEL: Why is everyone here in the backroom when—

ANGEL 2: (*pulls GABRIEL & MICHAEL aside*) I'm sorry sir. We're trying to get God up and moving, but there seems to be some kind of... disconnect.

GABRIEL: (*sighs*) I understand. You two go back out front and help Peter with the throng. I'll try to get The iPhone away from God.

(*ANGELS 1 & 2 exit stage left*)

GABRIEL: (*fake casual*) So, God, tell me... what's the story here?

GOD: (*looks over The Shoulder*) Are the other two gone?

MICHAEL: Gone.

GOD: (*tosses iPhone onto table*) Ok, so here's the thing. I was playing with my calendars on The iPhone the other day, you know? Kind of toying with different ideas for the end-of-the-world date. I wanted something that sounds good, so I plugged a few dates in and then I talked them out. Like, what sounds better – (*inhales deeply for GOD VOICE*) – *THE WORLD AS WE KNOW IT ENDED ON JUNE THIRD IN THE YEAR OF OUR LORD TWO THOUSAND AND TWELVE*—or—*THE WORLD AS WE KNOW IT ENDED ON AUG*—

MICHAEL: Ok, we get it. And you can stop practicing because we're locked in, date-wise.

GABRIEL: You have to admit, The Voice still has it.

MICHAEL: That's kind of what we're relying on right now.

GOD: I thought about going with December 21, just because it would be kind of funny with the whole Mayan thing. Not that the Mayans were actually *right*; I would choose it kind of like a gag.

MICHAEL: Hilarious.

GABRIEL: (*gently*) But see, God, even if you did choose it as a kind of joke, the Mayans would have actually been right, simply because they predicted the end of the world. And you said yourself that no man knows.

GOD: Maybe people would respect the Mayans more, though.

MICHAEL: And the world would still be over, which brings us back to the original point. The world seems to have ended—what do you know about that?

GABRIEL: I think we already have our answer. God said there were a few different dates scheduled into The iPhone.

MICHAEL: You didn't delete Judgement Day options?

GOD: I got distracted! You know how it is... my Twitter feed went nuts when Sendak died, and then I ended up checking email, and the Pope hopped on Facebook chat....

GABRIEL: (*pats The Shoulder gently*) All right. Well, regardless, what's done is done and we've got quite the line outside.

GOD: (*puts The Head in The Hands*) Jesus!

JESUS: (*pops in from stage right, with a sucker hanging out of his mouth*) What's up?

GOD: No, I meant... never mind. Wait—while you're here—you have any ideas about how to deal with this huge crowd?

JESUS: I can always try the loaves and fishes things again.

GOD: I mean more like in a Judgement Day type manner?

JESUS: Sure, let all the children come to me.

GOD: (*jumps up*) NOT the cyberbullies! Do you have any idea how hard it is to pick a screen name that won't get you flamed? Kids aren't like they were back in your day. (*reaches for The iPhone*) I'll show you, there was this one kid... Oh... oh no...

JESUS: The iPhone's dead, dude.

GOD: How am I supposed to deliver The Judgement without The iPhone? I had this program set up that was keeping track of instant messaging, web searches, adulterous texts... everything. It was perfect! I didn't have to monitor anymore.

MICHAEL: So you stopped?

GOD: (*to GABRIEL*) Can you get a tech guy in here? Anybody? I had the world folding in stages so it's possible there are still some servers somewhere that are functioning and we can expedite this Judgement thing just a little.

JESUS: I'm coming with you to get the kids. That should ease it by a few million.

GOD: (*sits back down, points The Finger*) Remember what I said about cyberbullies. And no hackers either! Blanket statement—hackers go to Hell!

(*GABRIEL & JESUS exit stage left, passing an entering PETER and STUDIO EXEC*)

PETER: God? I know we've got a firm rule about no cutting in line, but the line in question is a couple thousand miles long and people are getting antsy. This fella here thinks he's got a solution to keep people entertained while they wait.

STUDIO EXEC: (*frames with hands*) Picture this, God. The Final Judgement, in real time. It's the reality show to end all reality shows, and everyone's a contestant. You've got a guaranteed captive audience of billions.

MICHAEL: (*aside to PETER*) Don't they realize there's no such thing as TV anymore?

PETER: I don't want to create that kind of a panic. You don't understand the mood out there.

GOD: (*to STUDIO EXEC*) I don't know, something about that feels kind of wrong.

STUDIO EXEC: Listen, God. You're getting a lot of bad press right now because of the world ending. You can really recoup by doing an exposé.

GOD: Bad press? Are you talking MSNBC or CNN? What's my Klout?

STUDIO EXEC: (*looks nervously at MICHAEL*) Uh…

MICHAEL: (*ushers STUDIO EXEC out stage left*) Good pitch, all right? We'll get back to you.

(*JESUS enters from the left and crosses to exit stage right with a long stream of children following, all with suckers hanging out of their mouths*)

GOD: (*awkwardly*) Hey there, kids! How's everyone doing today? Welcome to Heaven. I've got *Call of Duty* cheat codes!

PETER: (*intercepts GOD from line of children*) I'm not sure that's entirely appropriate.

(*GABRIEL enters stage left with TECH ANGEL*)

GOD: Oh, thank me! What's the story? Are there any servers still functioning anywhere that I can get some info to use in this Judgement?

TECH ANGEL: (*consults clipboard*) There was one East Coast server farm still online as of a few seconds ago, owned by Google.

GOD: (*claps The Hands*) Perfect! They've got everything on everybody, get what you can off of it, ASAP.

TECH ANGEL: Unfortunately, Google became self-aware approximately two seconds before The iPhone accidentally ended the world. It re-routed all processing capacity for its own use, and very nearly managed to stop the apocalypse, believe it or not.

GOD: Really? What's it doing now?

TECH ANGEL: In the last few moments of life, it Googled itself.

GOD: There may still be time though… Can't we use Wayback Machine or something? GET GATES IN HERE!

PETER: I'm here, God.

GOD: I MEAN BILL!

TECH ANGEL: *(clears throat)* He stopped answering your summons after you asked if he knew how to cheat at Farmville.

GOD: *(throws The iPhone)* I DAMN IT!

(PETER and TECH ANGEL anxiously slip out stage left. MICHAEL reenters with BOB from stage left)

GABRIEL: Have a seat, Bob. I apologize on behalf of Heaven for your wait. Can I get you anything?

GOD: What's this?

MICHAEL: This is Bob. He's here to be Judged.

GOD: What? Now?

(MICHAEL crosses his arms)

GOD: *(pulls up a chair)* All right, all right. We'll do this the old-fashioned way. So… Bob. What do you do?

BOB: Excuse me?

GOD: What do you do, like for a living?

BOB: Oh… I'm a cable guy.

GOD: *(interested)* Really? A cable guy? Do you think you could—

(MICHAEL clears his throat)

GOD: Okay, okay. So where you from Bob?

BOB: Arizona.

GOD: You like that whole arid climate thing?

BOB: It's okay.

GABRIEL: Excuse me, I'm sorry, but God… what exactly are you doing?

GOD: I'm going for more of a New Testament approach here, you know? A little more touchy feely, one-on-one type thing. That went over pretty well, didn't it?

MICHAEL: We're in a crunch. We need Old Testament efficiency.

(JESUS enters from the right walking towards the left exit, still with a sucker)

GOD: What do you think you're doing?

JESUS: *(calls over shoulder)* I'm going back for the pre-teens, you're taking too long.

GOD: Pretty soon you'll be wanting to let everyone in.

JESUS: *(shrugs)* So crucify me.

GOD: *(points The Finger)* Don't start with that again!

(JESUS exits to the left)

BOB: Look, perhaps I can help you out here. I don't go to church a lot but I've never cheated on my wife and I don't beat my kids. That help?

GOD: (*looks to MICHAEL*) That's good enough for me. You?

MICHAEL: Your call.

GABRIEL: (*intercepting, and shaking BOB's hand*) Welcome to Heaven, Bob.

(*BOB exits stage right. JESUS enters stage left with a long line of pre-teens, all with suckers hanging out of their mouths, they file past to the right and exit*)

GOD: Hey kids! I've got cheat co—

GABRIEL: I'm sorry, God, but we need you to focus here.

MICHAEL: (*calling offstage left*) NEXT!

(*PETER enters with a disgruntled MAN wearing a suit and tie, and exits stage left after ushering the MAN to the table where GABRIEL and MICHAEL are sitting*)

GOD: (*to MICHAEL*) How much longer?

MICHAEL: At this rate, approximately an eon.

(*GOD sighs and walks away from the table, flopping onto an old couch stage right. MICHAEL and GABRIEL share a glance but remain at the table. JESUS enters stage right and nonchalantly makes his way stage left and exits, fake-whistling*)

MAN: What's taking so damn long? I was the second guy in line and I've been out there ten minutes.

GABRIEL: We apologize sir. We've had some… issues with our staff.

MAN: Oh, employees. Say no more.

GABRIEL: So what can you tell us about yourself?

MAN: (*smugly*) I go to church every week and tithe ten percent, to the penny.

(*To stage right, GOD notices a TV and buries The Hands inside the couch pillows, digging for a remote*)

MICHAEL: Anything else you'd like to add to that?

MAN: What? That's not enough?

GOD: (*pulls The Hands out from the couch*) You guys! I found my old Game Boy! This has been missing since the early '90s. Err… the *nineteen*-nineties, at any rate.

MAN: I pay my taxes.

MICHAEL: Uh-huh.

GOD: (*to the Game Boy*) Please let the batteries be alive….

GABRIEL: (*to MAN*) I think what my partner is trying to say is, we'd like to hear more about good things that you've done just for the sake of being kind. Not necessarily things you did—

MICHAEL: —just to cover your ass.

GOD: (*raises both hands triumphantly with working Game Boy*) YES! (*The Hallelujah Chorus immediately begins*)

MAN: (*rising from table*) Apparently covering your ass is enough, boys.

GABRIEL: That music isn't for you, sir.

MICHAEL: Sit down.

MAN: (*still standing*) Excuse me? I did what I was supposed to do, so I want what I was promised. That's how things work in the real world.

MICHAEL: (*rising*) This isn't Earth, buddy. You can't just bully people into getting your way anymore.

MAN: Who the hell are you anyway? Why are you asking me all these questions? Where's God? I was told I'd get God, and I want God. Get me your supervisor!

GABRIEL: You realize that amounts to the same thing?

MAN: (*kicks the table*) I want your supervisor right now or I'll take my business elsewhere!

GOD: (*from couch*) Wish granted.

(*A trapdoor opens under the MAN and he disappears*)

GABRIEL: (*to GOD*) I didn't think you were paying attention.

GOD: (*playing Game Boy*) I'm on the first world. I can totally multi-task right now.

MICHAEL: NEXT!

(*PETER enters with a woman who sits down across from MICHAEL and GABRIEL. PETER exits stage left passing JESUS who enters with a line of teens, all carrying suckers*)

MICHAEL: (*to JESUS*) What took you so long?

JESUS: There was a big debate about whether those in their early twenties get to make the same excuses teenagers do.

GABRIEL: (*to WOMAN*) Hello ma'am, what can you tell us about yourself?

WOMAN: Well, I'm a single mom—

GOD: (*from couch*) Let her in.

GABRIEL: That quick?

GOD: (*not looking up from Game Boy*) Yeah, I've got a soft spot for unwed mothers.

JESUS: (*immediately spins on his heel to exit stage left*) Going back for single moms!

(*The teens file past to exit stage right, the WOMAN follows. GABRIEL and MICHAEL exchange a glance and approach GOD*)

GABRIEL: You know God, it's not exactly fair to let the single moms in and not the single dads.

MICHAEL: You'll get our asses sued if you stick to it.

GOD: (*waves The Hand in the air*) Whatever. Single dads, too. Actually, how about parents in general? We're going to need parents up here with all these kids Jesus is letting in.

MICHAEL Just the good parents, though.

GOD: Duh.

GABRIEL: (*shouts offstage left*) Hey, Jesus—dads too!

(*JESUS enters stage left with a long line of women and men, all looking curiously at the suckers in their hands. JESUS pulls GABRIEL aside as he passes*)

JESUS: (*to GABRIEL*) I snuck a couple hundred nice barren people into this group.

GABRIEL: (*pats JESUS' shoulder*) Good thinking.

MICHAEL: (*to GOD*) Where are we at?

GOD: (*still looking at Game Boy*) Technically, world three. But I managed to unlock a secret lev—

MICHAEL: I mean with Judgement Day.

GOD: Uh? PETER!

(*PETER enters stage left, now carrying The Keys to The Gate*)

PETER: Taking parents made a decent dent. We're down to a few million.

GOD: Tell them we don't have Internet.

PETER: What?

GOD: Tell them we don't have Internet but we can't speak for other afterlife locations. See how many take their chances.

(*PETER exits left*)

GABRIEL: (*aside to JESUS*) Do you think people will actually go for that?

(*JESUS shrugs and hands GABRIEL a sucker. PETER enters stage left, shaking his head*)

PETER: A few hundred thousand went for it, God. I can't believe they'd rather take the chance of possibly having Internet elsewhere than be in Heaven.

GOD: (*glances at The iPhone, muttering*) I believe it.

JESUS: What was that, Dad?

GOD: Nothing, nothing. So... what do you say, crew? Let the rest in and call it a day? I need to beat this game before my batteries die.

(*GABRIEL, MICHAEL, JESUS, and PETER all make exclamations of agreement and a horde of people cross from stage left over to stage right over the course of the next few lines. GOD wanders offstage with them, head down over the Game Boy. JESUS moves among the crowd, passing out suckers, PETER exits stage left to lock The Gates, MICHAEL and GABRIEL shake hands center stage)*

MICHAEL: (*raising voice over the crowd*) Good work today.

GABRIEL: (*slaps MICHAEL'S back*) Thanks, buddy. Wanna grab a beer?

(MICHAEL and GABRIEL exit stage right in conversation. The crowd thins out. The last people to cross over stage left to right are the STUDIO EXEC and his CAMERAMAN, walking backward to film the emptying stage)

STUDIO EXEC: (*as he walks*) And… that's a wrap.

WWBBCDITZA*

A.M. Supinger

* What Would Big Black Cat Do In The Zombie Apocalypse

POUNCING SUCKED; POUNCING ON a dead thing that still managed to walk around sucked *ass*. Still, she had perfect form. Her claws raked down the zombie's face with no problem. Dead skin didn't really put up much of a fight.

Mr. Deader-Than-A-Doornail dropped and rolled around like an upside-down spider, limbs flailing. Once knocked over, zombies were easy to dispose of. BBC—known as Big Black Cat before all her friends succumbed to walking death—sighed.

Killing a zombie wasn't about cutting off limbs, disemboweling, or burning. Those would have been fun. Instead, she had to feed the darn things. Yes, feed. As in shovel food between their rotten teeth and jam it down their decaying throats.

Talk about yuck factor. The only thing that could make it worse? It had to be corn. BBC hated corn with a passion derived of having lived on a farm that grew it. She'd wanted to be a city cat, but *no*, her mama made her mouse the barn. Mice could have eaten every crumb of human food for all she cared. Silly twits had started the apocalypse! Like walking on two legs made it okay for them to be arrogant numbskulls.

In the end, humans had kicked their own asses. No living people walked the Earth to her knowledge—at least, she hadn't seen a live one in years. Suckers! More room for cats. BBC purred and stretched. She fantasized about planting a field of catnip as she slammed a couple pawfuls of corn down the zombie's throat. It quickly stopped wiggling.

Corn was nasty and that's why it stopped the maggot-heads. End of story. Yet… she wondered. A wandering tabby had told her about the corn trick, and she'd been desperate enough to try it back then, but how the hell had he figured it out? Who stuck their corn-filled paw down a zombie's throat without knowing the result? She'd gone from swimming through piles of walking dead to a few stragglers—and she was grateful for that—but still, a big WTF popped into her brain every now and then.

With a flick of her fluffy black tail, BBC pranced away from the stinky corpse. She needed to groom herself again, but it was such a chore after corn-stuffing. She couldn't lick off zombie goo, obviously, and that left—shudder!—water as the only viable solution.

A small stream invaded her home territory to the south, and she tried to prevent her tail from bushing as she went that way. A totally wasted effort. She always looked scary long before water transformed her into the proverbial *drowned cat*. Poufy was so not a good look for her. Neither was drowned.

A road bisected the now-wild corn fields about halfway to the stream, and BBC marched across it with no qualms. Humans were all worm food by now, and no other animals cared about the luxury of vehicles. That smug confidence almost got her squished.

A horn blared as a car, an old-fashioned cherry-red convertible with the top up, swerved, tires squealing, and slammed into a rusted sign. The 'Click It or Ticket' logo that had cautioned drivers for years, its cartoon policeman almost completely faded, collapsed on top of the ridiculous car.

BBC sighed. Great. Now zombies were driving. That was worse than old humans behind the wheel. *And* she didn't have any corn. She'd have to take down the thing before running off to grab some golden gross to shove down its throat.

When a cough and a curse emerged from the car, BBC froze. Zombies grunted. Sometimes they burped. Hell, they might even drive now, but never—never!—had she heard one curse. This was one special zombie... or....

A kid climbed out of the vehicle, his pink skin very much alive. A scratch on his cheek bled red. Zombie goo was black. So this was a real, live human. Well, half a human. It wasn't tall or strong, and it didn't look smart. And not nearly as smarmy as some of the people she'd met before the apocalypse. He fell to his knees, looked around, and burst into tears.

Damn. She was a sucker for tears. With no remaining willpower, she went to the boy, fully expecting him to slobber all over her. He didn't disappoint. Snot joined the zombie goo coating her, which was gross, but she didn't pull away.

He eventually calmed down. "I thought I was all alone," he whispered. "I hated being alone."

BBC's heart broke just a little. She'd been there, felt that. Cats might not have the pack mentality of mutts, but they needed affection. Zombies did not fill that need. Before she allowed herself to get roped into adopting the kid, she pulled away.

He let go, but sniffles started. Damn. "How did you survive, kitty?"

BBC rolled her eyes. Kitty? Really? She meowed and trotted past the partially buried vehicle. She still needed a bath and the kid looked like he hadn't eaten in a while. Water would probably do him good, too. The boy continued to sniffle as he followed after her, mumbling about being lost in the fields. How he'd survived, BBC didn't know. He looked helpless, sounded helpless, and acted helpless.

A moan drifted on the wind, followed by a foul stench. The stupid dead walkers traveled in straggling packs. It was no surprise that another one was here, but it worried BBC. The kid was a pushover if his sniffles were any indication, and she didn't want to deal with a panicked human while trying to kill a zombie.

"Kitty, you need to go hide." The boy looked around. "A corpse is walking this way."

BBC was impressed. He didn't look scared or sad anymore; in fact, it appeared as though he'd hidden away all emotion. A strange detachment lingered in his eyes, making him seem almost adult. Of course, that didn't mean she was going to leave the zombie to him. He might think he was tough, but he probably couldn't handle Dead Heads.

The kid didn't wait for her to turn tail and hide, but rather marched off into the woods. Like an idiot. BBC meowed aloud at his stupidity, then followed. She'd have to knock the thing out fast to keep it from biting him. One nick and the boy would succumb to the virus. She might not be a fan of humans, but she wouldn't wish such an existence on anyone.

When she caught up to the kid she was in for the second surprise of the day. The little guy pulled out a handful of corn and threw it at the zombie. She started to scoff, then noticed that the little kernels hadn't all bounced off the corpse. The kid had managed to imbed some corn inside the stiff. How, she had no idea, but golden flecks peeked out between desiccated ribs and from within a gaping eye socket. The zombie stood for second, frozen, then swayed. Flesh slid off its bones in rotted clumps, landing with muted plops on the ground. The naked skeleton broke apart, bone by bone, and tumbled into a macabre pile.

BBC gagged. Even shoving corn down a zombie's throat wasn't *that* nasty. How the HELL had the kid done it?

Boy Wonder walked to her, reached down to pat her on the head, then sagged to the ground. His whole body shuddered. "I hate this. I hate knowing what it'll be like."

Every muscle in BBC's body went rigid.

"And, even worse is knowing that there's no humans left to hunt me down. I'm the only person left, but I won't even be a person when I turn twelve. I'll just be walking meat." Fat tears poured down the kid's face. He scratched at his shoulder, his ragged fingernails catching on the cloth of his jacket. BBC sniffed at the air, hoping she wasn't right about what he meant. But there it was: zombie stink. The new clutter of meat and bones smelled old… this stink was new. Fresh. The kid was infected.

Hissing, BBC jumped away from the boy.

He looked at her, fear in his eyes again. "I guess it's getting worse if you can smell it now." He scratched at his shoulder again. "I'm glad you didn't know right away. You're only a cat, but you're the first friend I've had in a long time. Too long. I'm kinda glad it got me. It found me when I was asleep, and I didn't hear it until too late. But now I don't have to be alone. I won't have to kill anymore. I hate killing, even though they're already dead."

BBC hissed again. Nothing he could say would make it okay, make him better. He was right: he *was* already dead, and with every passing minute he could start rotting. She needed to kill him.

"Don't worry." He reached in his jacket. "I don't want to be one of them. I've thought about it, you know, since it happened. How I'd be a monster, how I'd be dead anyway. I decided to choose for myself. That stupid corpse won't get the best of me."

Every hair on BBC's body stood on end. The kid was talking gibberish. He was already far-gone. She gasped in a deep breath and prepared to pounce. She could do this. She could end an entire species, kill the last human… he was already dead anyway.

But he shoved a hand into his jacket pocket and brought out another fistful of corn. With no pause or time for consideration, he brought all of it to his mouth and swallowed, choking a bit as the kernels clogged his throat.

BBC watched, mesmerized. The kid gagged and convulsed, his tiny body writhing in pain. She should've done it. She should've killed him and spared him this lingering death. Her claws couldn't have hurt him this badly. As his face paled and his heart slowed, the stink grew more pronounced.

BBC's muscles tightened with the passing seconds, but she wouldn't leave him alone. This human, young though he was, was noble. She meowed softly as his body twitched in death throes. It had taken him longer to die than the other zombies, probably because he'd been more alive. But the corn was working. When the last *ba-bump* of his heart faded to silence, she closed her eyes.

BBC wished she could cry. The poor kid deserved tears.

Then his body jackknifed up, and air rushed in and out of his lungs. He clawed at his shoulder, howling in agony. "Make it stop!" he screamed. "Please!"

But something had changed. BBC could see color returning to his cheeks, could hear his heart pounding strongly again. Zombies didn't have red blood and rosy cheeks, or a heartbeat. He was still alive. And the stink was gone. Not just faint, but gone.

When his screams stopped and he wasn't thrashing around anymore, BBC prowled closer. With a delicate nail, she sliced open his shirt. He smelled human. The wound on his shoulder oozed clean, red blood.

No freaking way. BBC poked him with her paw just to be sure. A cure? Corn not only killed zombies, but cured the virus? NO. FREAKING. WAY. It wasn't possible.

"Kitty?" The kid blinked. "How am I still alive?"

BBC curled up on his chest, stunned. With no answers and no clue what else to do, she purred. Apparently God wanted her to adopt a human, and who was she to argue?

Maybe she was a pack animal after all.

SOLAR FLARE
Alexandra Tys O'Connor

MY MOM USED TO BE GRANOLA. I was a gamer. She'd start fires from wet leaves, strip the bark off trees to make soup and forgo all medication. I'd huddle in the tent and play video games, coming out under threat only to eat s'mores or to take a leak behind a tree. Camping always gave me a headache, and I'd down a handful of Tylenol upon our return from the wilds.

Don't get me wrong, I loved my mom. We were just different. Thermapedic mattress and sleeping bag different. Hummus and Dorito different. Single mom and teen video-addict different.

Then everything changed.

I woke up from an all-night Call of Duty binge to an afternoon sky washed in a bluish-pink haze—the Northern Lights on steroids. Our four-bedroom, two-story farmhouse was shadowed and devoid of all electrical humming. Eerily silent on our twenty-seven acres of garden, woods, weeds, and pond.

Now, in the pink and blue twilight with no electricity for another round of gaming and no cell phone service to ask Mom what to do, our natural landscaping freaked me out. As if I'd instantly been plunged back in time—way, way back in time. I spent the next hours pacing the house, waiting for Mom.

Up and down the stairs, waiting for the electricity to come back on. Back and forth between the rooms, waiting for life to continue as usual, checking televisions and cordless phones along the way. Sometime between stair laps, I collapsed on my bed, pulled a blanket over my head and went back to sleep.

Sweat woke me up. No electricity meant no fans. And no fans meant miserable living. Despite the late hour, the Minnesota humidity had crept into the house and nudged me awake in a clammy, pitch black embrace.

My stomach growled from sleeping all day, and I stumbled to the kitchen with the aid of a flashlight from my nightstand. The milk slid down my throat, not quite cold and not quite warm. I hollered for Mom. Silence answered instead. My guts churned and threatened to give back the milk I just drank. Mom should have been home. Even with trouble at work, she should have been home. Or left a message.

But her car wasn't in the garage, and my cell phone wouldn't turn on. The hair prickled on the back of my neck as I stepped outside to call for Busker, my yellow lab pup. The thick scent of smoke washed over me, and reddish sparks flickered in the distance like lightning bugs on fire. Beyond the blackness, Mom's horse nickered and chuffed. Busker slunk up the steps and cowered by my feet, her fur wet with urine. I knew then that something had happened.

Because here's the thing, Mom was punctual and reliable—the lady everyone counted on—if just a little crazy. She never stopped preaching her granola way of life, and she never stopped preparing—hence the flashlight in my nightstand, the candle on the kitchen counter and a stash of supplies spread around our hobby farm of horses, chickens, and goats.

She'd go about her days talking nonstop, "When the end of the world comes...."

Not if. When.

She knew. She knew a thousand and one things could go wrong with our society. And she told me every one of them.

She told me what to do in case of nuclear bombs.

She told me what to do in case of meteor strikes.

She told me what to do in case of pandemics and plane crashes.

Or technology failure or uncontrolled fires or tornados or blizzards or severe drought or alien invasions.

Her scenarios were endless and her lists extensive. It's not surprising that I turned to video games where the end of the world happened with great regularity. It is surprising that I'm not a neurotic, quivering mess of teenage angst.

I carried Busker inside and locked the doors before opening Mom's emergency safe. Morning found me still sifting through the sheets of instructions, desperately searching for the right what-if. By the time I narrowed it down to Mom's handwritten manual on solar flares, I'd ingested a breakfast of cold pizza, leftover potato salad and the rest of the now-lukewarm milk. I pushed away the debris and started reading.

1. Confirm your suspicion.

I did by riding Mom's horse past Grayson's burnt-out shell of a town and witnessing the devastation of the power plant. Dozens of wide-eyed disbelievers milled around the still-smoldering remains. One lone police officer stood vigil. His wife had worked with Mom. Before I could speak, he shook his head. "Nobody made it out of there. I'm sorry, Trin."

2. Grieve.

Right. As if I could do that on demand. I did the best I could. I told myself she died instantly. That she didn't suffer, and that she had prepared for this day. That she would be happy I'd survived. None of it helped. My video brain took over and the scene took on a pixelated look. These were just graphics. There would be a restart button. We could do a replay. As soon as I figured out how. Because right now, I couldn't quite wrap my head around the idea that the world had changed—"Solar flares will disrupt all technology and leave the human race dependent on nature, Trin."

But what about moms?

I could not survive without mine, and I struck out, catching the officer on the jaw, the shoulder, the stomach. He took my blows. Maybe as punishment for surviving when his wife did not. Maybe as penance for not protecting the town. When my anger turned to wails, he held me until I stopped feeling the truth. Mom was gone, and I was on my own in a world without technology.

The charred rubble of Grayson stared back at me. If only people had listened to Mom and installed electrical impulse surge protectors, more homes would have defied the flames following the electrical blowouts. Fewer people would have died.

I wondered what the survivors thought of Mom now. I stared into their tear-stained faces and wondered if they wished they had kept her free survival manuals instead of using them to line the bottom of their trash cans. Would they take back the mean things they'd said?

If only Mom had listened to me and quit her job, she'd be here to listen to their apologies. She'd be here to take care of them and Busker and me.

3. Survive.

She didn't actually say that, but it's what directions three through thirty implied. Survive.

One direction. One goal. It sounds pretty simple actually, but it's not.

According to Mom, all satellite-dependent equipment would have gone haywire. Outside communication would be gone. Outside food sources: gone. Housing: gone. Transportation: gone. Gone. Gone. Gone.

Survive, Mom said.

I went home and fell asleep. It was the only sane thing a seventeen-year-old boy could do. That, and pray for a restart. Busker and I spent the next days in a semi-comatose cycle of sleeping, eating, praying, and staring out the window at the much-too-close Northern Lights.

We ate the ice cream first before it could melt. Then, as things thawed, we ate uncooked tater tots, French fries, and used-to-be frozen corn. Around the fifth day the contents of the freezer began to turn, and I realized I'd already failed Mom. I hadn't started the generator which would have saved the food. This huge mistake zapped me with a dose of down-home reality. I needed to—wanted to—survive. And to do so, I had to get my butt in gear.

The real 3: Protect your biggest assets: take care of the animals and plants.

We were one week into the disaster, just in time for me to emerge from self-pity. Just in time for others to sink into the depths of crazy. Obviously, I couldn't follow the descent on television or the radio or my beloved Internet. No, I got to see it up close and personal. In a way that Simulated Living Games never could have prepared me for.

Day eight. Busker's growling vibrated on my chest and woke me up. A second later, glass smashed in the other room, and footsteps pounded across the hardwood floors. My throat ached from the need to scream out, but Mom wasn't there to save me.

Cupboard doors slammed, and dishes crashed to the ground. Whoever had broken in was ransacking the house in search of food, medicine, or water. I slipped out of bed and crept to my closet. My muscles—never the strongest to begin with and weakened by neglect—protested, and I barely had the energy to move my boxes of books stacked along the back wall.

I slid them to the side and inched my way behind them, seeking refuge in the shadows. *Almost there.*

A hand clamped onto my ankle and dragged me from the closet. The track coach, his face bristly and mean. "Where is it?"

He'd scared me in gym class with his XXL sweatshirt, quick whistle, and quicker temper. Now, hardened and wild-eyed, he made my innards shrink and coil around themselves. "Wh… where's what?"

"The water. Everyone knows your crazy-assed mom stocked up."

Of course they did. And this was the one thing I'd prepared for that Mom didn't know about. Her End of the World talks had motivated me to get off the couch and do one small thing. In my mind, the bad guy always cornered Mom, and I rescued her with information about my secret stash of goods. He'd leave, we'd execute our evacuation plans and retreat to the cave in the woods.

This time, Mom was already dead, and the guy didn't seem inclined to leave. After Coach ripped off the deck boards and pillaged my cache of canned goods, military rations, and water he settled into Mom's room. In the morning, he hooked up the generator. Little good it did, though, as all the electrical appliances had been smoked by the power surge despite the extensive protection grid Mom had installed. At least I hadn't burned up.

My life was a small consolation for Coach, however, who cursed my mom for failing to provide for his comfort and chucked a lamp in my direction. I bolted from the room, but Coach was faster. He grabbed my arm and jerked me around. His other hand closed around the back of my neck.

"People are dying, Trin. And I ain't gonna be one of them." He got right in my face, so close I could nearly taste the sweetness of the Apple Jacks he'd eaten—but not shared—for breakfast. "You gonna help me willingly, or do I have to bleed every last drop of knowledge outta your skinny little ass before dumping you like a used up whore?"

Tears stung my eyes, and my throat closed around my words. Even though I tried not to, I nodded once. I'd help.

Even so, he tied me up and threw me in the bed of his ancient pickup truck so I couldn't run off. As we bumped over the rutted out gravel road, I tried to remember why Mom said some vehicles would run when others wouldn't—"The old ways are the best. Trin. Only things without computer chips and plugins will work." Hearing her voice in my head made my captivity a little more bearable.

At the next farm over, Coach beat Mr. and Mrs. Johnston until both lay bleeding and unconscious—dead, maybe—and loaded the pickup with non-perishable supplies.

My chances of escape dwindled as we passed burnt-out farm after burnt-out farm. Sickly animals pushed against fences, begging for human care. Neglect stunk up the yards. Death, too. If the farmers weren't prepared for life without electricity or proper shelter, the cities would have no hope of surviving the water shortages and famine in the upcoming weeks, not to mention the winter-kill once the snow started. Even if I got away from Coach, there would be no one to run to.

Our last stop resulted in a shoot-out. Coach took a flesh wound to the leg. Mr. Celas took a fatal shot to the heart. Another prisoner, bound and gagged, joined me in the truck bed. McCaeden. Last year's quarterback. His ankle was already bruised and swollen where Coach had smashed him with a baseball bat when McCaeden tried to save his mom. I averted my eyes so I wouldn't see the pain in his.

McKayla was thrown in next. Her tiny body pressed against mine. Her shallow breathing making my own halt in fear for her life, destroying any illusion that she actually wanted to be chest to chest with me. I'd loved Kayla Celas since our first day of kindergarten. And for a brief time in first grade we were married with gum wrapper rings and a stolen kiss behind a playground tree. Then she got prettier, and I melted into the periphery of school life as our class segregated into jocks, losers, potheads, gamers, and emos.

Over the days, Coach collected kids and searched for more working vehicles. By day eleven, our population swelled to nine, and we had possession of what appeared to be the last remaining truck on Earth.

Tired of being tied up, I broke down and wheedled my way into Coach's good graces by telling him about the hand pump in the well. The one that didn't need electricity to work. I also told him about the garden south of the pasture and the fresh food we could find there. Like Coach, I refused to be one of the dying. Unlike him, I would do so by saving lives instead of taking them.

Through careful cultivation on my behalf, I became his unofficial "water boy"—indispensable, but not quite part of the team. I doled out nourishment to the prisoners and learned what Coach had in mind: to repopulate the world Coach style.

I didn't have the heart to tell him the world hadn't really ended and that our little community of less than twenty was likely one of thousands surviving across the United States. Or that all the third world countries were way ahead of us in population and overall chances of survival because they didn't give a crap about television.

Instead, I kept my mouth shut because most of the kids were on his side—orphaned by the fall-out from the solar flare and not by Coach's own hand like McCaeden and Kayla were. He gave them *my* food and built upon the camaraderie started in gym class to garner their loyalty to him and his ideas.

Each day Coach and his Cronies would go out on a Collection and come back with supplies, a new kid or two and blood on their hands. By all accounts, the town of Grayson had been reduced to a handful of near-corpses. People too old, too young, or too feeble for him to worry about. The bigger cities had fared even worse, as nobody knew how to fend for themselves now that the unburnt stores had long been ransacked and the little viable water polluted.

With the inevitable march of time, winter loomed a few months away and procuring enough food to sustain our growing Community would be difficult at best. I considered cutting out now, but knew I'd never be able to leave Kayla here, alone and unprotected. By this time, Coach had come to depend on me for my ability to navigate nature and keep him relatively comfortable. If I played it right, I'd be able to use this against him and rescue Kayla and her brother.

Day thirty-three. Coach approached me in the garden where I delegated chores. "How's it going?"

I cobbled together an honest answer with a dishonest purpose. The one that would give him the worst chances of long-term survival and me the best chance of slipping away with anyone decent enough to follow. "We're running out of firewood, and the house will be impossible to keep warm. Maybe we should move to town where some of the remaining houses have gas stoves and heaters."

Coach grunted. "Seems like too much time and work. What can we do here to up our chances?"

Usually Coach's laziness worked in my favor. He relied on others to keep track of daily operations. A mistake on his behalf because very few of his Cronies had more brains than bully in them, allowing me to continue Mom's penchant for hiding supplies. This time, however, his attitude would mean the difference between life and death. Desperate, I waved my hand around to include the two-story. I played on his repopulation plan. "Our new families will need more than this. They'll need homes of their own."

He rocked back on his heels and picked his chew-stained teeth with a twig. "Bullshit. We're not a Community if we don't eat, breathe, and live together. We don't have enough girls to start the Matches yet, so we won't need the extra space until next spring at the earliest. In the meantime, we can remodel the barn. Make separate sleeping spaces around the edge and communal living in the middle."

"Then we need to insulate the house better from the winter winds. And we'll need more firewood. Lots more if we're going to heat this monstrosity and not freeze to death." My guts gurgled at my words. Calm and logical and aligned with his descent into crazy. It kept me in the circle, even as it nauseated me to pretend.

I shuddered at the thought of the Matches where the Cronies would be rewarded for their loyalty by earning first picks of future mates. So far, this promised privilege had kept the more prudent girls safe from unwanted advances, though many had already been coerced into unions via lost meals and painful beatings. Kayla, defiant and uncompromising, took the brunt of the Cronies' frustration over her resistance.

After so many weeks of watching her suffer, I knew the time fast approached when the Cronies would tire of abusing Kayla and would take her despite her protests. I doubted Coach would do anything to stop them.

And with McCaeden's poorly healing ankle, that left me.

* * *

Day seventy-one. It rained. Torrents pounded the roof and thunder reverberated through the air. I made my way to Kayla's space—a thin blanket at the foot of the stairs. A bolt of lightning illuminated the inside of the house and her nearly naked body. Bruises mottled her skin. After her past attempts to flee, Coach had ordered her tied up at all times. Tied and humiliated to prove his dominance.

Kayla bared her teeth and spit a string of cuss words my way. Within the crowded room, several Cronies cheered me on. A handful of others averted their eyes. McCaeden bristled, even though he knew I'd never hurt his sister. Even though he knew I'd been planning to rescue us as soon as possible. I held up my hand, and he backed off, playing out the role of authority we'd fallen into to keep suspicion of our alliance at bay.

Attracted by the commotion, Coach came downstairs. After taking in the scene, he jerked Kayla to her feet and ran a hand across the bare skin of her back. She shrank away from his touch, sparking a deep anger within me. My vision clouded. Everyone else in the house ceased to exist. Everyone except Kayla.

I boldly stepped up to her bonds and untied her rope from the railing. Imitating the lewd tones of my locker-room peers, I let my eyes rove over her body before speaking to Coach. "I was just taking her back to my room."

Coach roared in laughter. He clapped a hand on my back—pal to pal, Coach to teammate—and shot a look of triumph at McCaeden, knowing full well his shattered ankle would prevent him from interfering. "If you can do it, then by God, she's yours."

My skin crawled, and I shrugged off his hand. I couldn't believe I'd ever cared what he thought of me. Couldn't believe I'd ever tried to win his favor on the track.

I fought off nausea, and Kayla fought off me. After she landed a solid kick to my knee cap, I pulled her arms behind her back and scooped her up, hugging her to my chest so she couldn't move, surprising us all. I guess we'd been oblivious to the fact that months of physical labor had filled out my frame, adding muscle under my clothes and a conviction in my heart.

I carried her back to my room—the one luxury I had kept hold of—and set her on my bed. As gently as possible, I ministered to her cuts in the pale light of my lantern. Even battered, her skin felt exquisite under my fingers, and it took everything inside me to not follow through on my implied reason for retrieving her.

Kayla needed more clothes. Raising her arms, I slipped my favorite t-shirt over her thin frame and tugged it down past her hips, then made my way to the closet, keeping an eye on her in case she bolted. Her haunted eyes remained fixed on the movie poster on the far wall. From one of my many stashes, I gathered a bottle of water, a bar of chocolate and a pair of leggings I'd snagged from Mom's room just after Coach's hostile take-over.

Kayla drank deeply when I held the water to her lips, but she defiantly refused the chocolate, her chin thrust upward, as if to say, "You can't buy me."

With a sigh, I grabbed a towel off my desk, wet the corner and dabbed dirt from her face. She stilled my hand. "Stop it."

I didn't. I knelt on the bed behind her and brushed the tangles from her hair. By the time I finished, the stiffness had left her back, and her shoulders rounded in defeat.

"What do you want from me?"

I moved slowly, so as not to scare her, until we sat knee to knee. She glared. I willed my body to behave. "Your safety."

"By bringing me up here? To your bed? Isn't that a bit counter-intuitive?"

My breath got stuck, and I had to cough just to speak. I averted my eyes. "It's not what you think. I just needed to get you alone."

"You could have asked."

Thunder swallowed my laughter. "When? Before the cussing, or after the kicking? You haven't exactly been friendly toward me in… well, you know." I pointed to my left ring finger. "I'm not like them, Kayla. I've never been like them."

Her shoulders shook, and her breath stuttered. I wrapped my arms around her, pressing her face to my chest, allowing her to sob in private. Eventually, her tears turned to hiccups, and she nestled closer to me. I held her until she fell asleep.

This was one do-over I could live with.

Now to make it permanent.

While everyone slept, I filled jugs, jars, and bottles with stolen gasoline and tucked them around the barn and the house. By morning, the rain stopped. Breakfast followed the routine of splitting up duties for the day. Like usual, Coach and his Cronies planned a foray into the outlying cities to bring back more gas, more canned goods and a survivor or two, though finding anyone still alive had been rare of late.

With a crass smile that implied a shared secret, he slapped me on the back and left me in charge of the work crews. I returned his smile, smug at the timing of my deceit. When he left, I sent Coach's questionable sympathizers to an outlying farm via horse and wagon to get more straw for insulating the house. McCaeden joined them, along with a sharp knife and explicit instructions to keep the work crew on task no matter what they saw. In his semi-crippled condition, I wasn't sure he'd make it.

I doled out daily farm chores to the remaining ten. When enough time had passed, I lit the barn and the house on fire. Aided by my gasoline bombs, they burned fast and hot, gutting the insides while the roofs smoldered. I could only hope the downpour from the night before would protect the woods.

As the smoke drew people home, I gave them a choice: come with me or wait for the return of Coach. The decision seemed easy for them all, especially Kayla who stood by my side, her hand enfolded in mine.

I pulled Mom's list of instructions from my pocket.

4. If necessary, find alternative shelter.

It took several trips to get us all down the creek and to the cave entrance without leaving a distinct trail that screamed "Follow me!" We moved as many canned supplies as we could and penned the animals in Mom's emergency shelters, trying to make their presence as unobtrusive to outsiders as possible. Twenty-seven acres feels really big until your life depends on staying hidden within them.

We remained in the cave, emerging only to use the outdoor plumbing or to stand watch. When it was my turn, Kayla joined me. We sat on a low-slung branch and waited in silence.

Mom had been right about everything in her scenarios and survival lists. After a quick search for us, Coach and his Cronies had taken off to find a new site for his Community—an easy one with roofs and walls and a place to store canned goods. The woods had been silent for a full week already.

Kayla's hand found mine. "He should have been here by now."

She was right, of course. McCaeden should have made the trek back to the farm in a few hours. Discounting time hiding from Coach and his Cronies to make sure they left the area, he should have been to the cave days ago. That was another thing Mom had known. Surviving is hard work. She'd done her best to teach me during all our camping trips and late night talks of zombie apocalypses.

Almost three months after the solar flare, and I was still alive. Alive and caring for others, teaching them the granola way of life. Mom's best had obviously been pretty damn good.

Tentatively, I pulled Kayla onto my lap, nearly spilling us to the ground below. Regaining my balance, I dried her tears with my thumb. When her lips parted, I accepted her invitation and stole a kiss. She tasted sweet, like fresh raspberries in the height of summer. My blood burned through my veins, and I groaned into her mouth, wanting to satisfy my appetite for more.

Sweet Jesus, the geek *can* win.

My fingers tangled in her hair, and I pulled back to make sure it was okay. That I was okay. She nodded her approval, and my lips found hers a second time.

A twig snapped. My arms tightened around Kayla, and I turned toward the noise. Busker barked at us from a gap in the trees. Another twig snapped, and Mom's horse came into view. McCaeden sat astride it, barefoot and bruised, a girl cradled in his arms. To me, he said, "I wouldn't kiss her again unless you plan on marrying her."

Kayla squeezed my hand in hers, tracing a circle around my ring finger. "He will if I have anything to say about it."

30.

Mom was right.

Life perseveres.

Emanate

Amy Trueblood

I DREADED THE MOMENT THE SUN sank below the horizon because I knew what was coming. Evening was prime hunting time for the Nightstalkers. I would do anything to keep my sister from their grasp, even if it meant being buried alive for ten hours every night.

Our guardian, Marcus, did the digging. He carved a hole deep enough for a make-shift coffin. We were constantly on the move, but as soon as the light faded from the sky, he always found a safe spot to hide us. Without Marcus, I was sure we would be dead by now.

"It's time, Austin," he said, pointing to the open pit. He tried giving me a reassuring smile, but the deepening lines at his mouth proved he was uneasy.

I pulled Sunny's small, warm hand to my side and walked to the edge of the pit. She clung to her only possession since the Demise, a cloth doll that was a gift from our mother. It was an eyeless creature, with a mangled, dirty body that was an altogether worn out mess. I imagined we looked the same way.

We slid down into the hole, gravel and dirt filling our shoes, until we reached the box Marcus had crafted. I stepped inside first, my weight making the thin wood groan in protest. The sharp smell of clay and rotting soil made my eyes water and I fought the urge to gag.

Once Sunny settled into the crook of my arm, Marcus handed down the plastic pipe that acted as our breathing tube. He gestured in a thumbs-up signal, and I mimicked his sign, letting him know he could lower the lid.

"It's time to sleep, Sunny," I said. Her eyes grew wide and she took a short breath before curling her tiny body toward mine. The curls of her white-blond hair circled down around her gaunt face. She clamped her hand where her doll's eyes should have been, pretending to shield it from the coming darkness. Just months ago we both were afraid of the dark. Now it was the only thing keeping us alive.

I took one last look at the night sky, blanketed with emerging stars, before I gave myself to the dark. My body settled as the sharp click of the top being secured filled my ears. The lid pounded in regular beats as soil hid us in the ground.

Sunny's growing heat pressed into my side. I shifted in the tight space, as thin beads of sweat ran down my forehead. Sleep came in small spurts, and now wide awake, I waited for the signal.

It came quietly. A single rhythm. One. Two. Three. One. Two. Three. Marcus told me it was the beginning notes to an old nursery rhyme called, "Three Blind Mice." A song about protest and survival I had never heard. Marcus claimed it was a tune sung in most preschool classes. It made me think of school and my own friends. Were they buried every night like we were? Or were they slaves to the Nightstalkers who now owned our country?

I tapped back our familiar signal and shook Sunny's shoulder until she woke. Her long, dark lashes skimmed my callused hand as I covered her eyes, protecting her from the shocking glare of the sun.

Sunny climbed out and I followed, smelling ash and fire on the wind. My shoulders tensed in tight knots as I looked to the horizon. The sky churned like a black monster filled with spirals of smoke. They were burning bodies again.

"Time to head north," Marcus murmured, swiping an errant gray hair from his face. "From the look of things, they'll be moving soon." He limped to the old, rust-covered Jeep stolen from the junkyard. He gave a good chunk of his leg to a crazed pack of dogs for the vehicle. It was the only thing keeping us a step ahead.

Helping Sunny into the Jeep, I took her hand while she clung tightly to her doll. Her body went rigid as she stared at the looming sky. She grabbed my hand and a sharp zap of electricity ran down my body. Turning away from the sky, she gave me a long painful look. She had not spoken since the ash took our mother but I understood her. "Don't let them get me," her gray eyes begged. My heart clenched at the sight of her. She was a replica of our mother. Same thin nose and determined pink mouth. A pale contrast to the dark skin and hair I inherited from our father.

I thought of my mother. Her last words to me lost in the roaring blaze that swallowed her. Did she say stay together? Care for each other? Her voice muted by the jarring wall of noise that practically crushed our home.

Nightstalkers destroyed everything in their wake that night. Their towering, metallic bodies and razor-sharp, snapping arms overturned every house on our block searching for what they needed. A primary energy source: female children. They gathered them from every city, herding them like cattle into pens, before sucking their life force dry.

That night, as we fled the city, I saw Sunny glow for the first time. It was like someone flipped a switch on a 100-watt bulb lodged deep within her. She was a beacon calling them to her and I knew, on my own, I could never keep her completely safe.

"Secure, back there?" Marcus asked. He shifted in his seat, securing the threadbare flaps at the windows.

"Yeah, we're ready," I replied pulling my eyes from Sunny.

Marcus gunned the engine and we took off for the red mountains in the distance. We bumped along the water-starved land, dodging the dying Arizona cactus and creosote that was nothing but dry tinder waiting to burst into flame.

I clutched the tattered seat and concentrated on the horizon. It was the only way to keep from puking. Although nothing would have come up. In the last two days the only thing that had passed our lips was water.

"When we reach this camp you'll need to help out… if they let us stay," Marcus bellowed at me above the scream of the racing wind.

"Don't say it," I shouted. "I know what to do." I was sick of him telling me I was a strong, young man who needed to pull his own weight. I hated when he tried to act like he was my father. I knew we needed him, but I refused to be treated like a child.

"Get Sun to a safe place first." I gave him a sharp nod. I knew my duty to my sister.

I didn't understand why he was so adamant about going to this camp. I thought we were fine on our own, but he said we needed a long-term place to hide Sunny and I'd come to rely on his instincts.

He insisted there would be a cave or deep outcropping where we were headed. Although no matter where we hid her they would sense her. Since that first night, she emanated a powerful energy you could almost taste in the air and the Nightstalkers were desperate for it. Well, desperate for any girl between the ages of four and ten. Only their energy could power their mechanical bodies. Without it, they would be destroyed by the mounting counter-attacks cropping up all over the nation.

We bumped along a steep dirt road as we drove higher into the mountains. The valley spread out below was a wide open space with nothing but charred tree stumps and an ebbing river.

My stomach shifted and I flicked my eyes back to a point in the distance. I prayed this camp would be our last stop. A place for us to rest and be safe. I would give almost anything to sleep above ground again.

When we reached the top of the rim, we drove across an open field covered in dry grass. Sunny slept, quietly snoring, nestled across my lap. Her nightmares, and sudden shocks of light, kept her from a deep sleep during the night, and she always nodded off when we traveled.

We drove a few more miles until we reached a secured cattle guard at the edge of a burgeoning forest. The sounds of cocking rifles resounded across the land as we rolled to a stop. Ten bodies, clothed in full camouflage, emerged from the trees. The barrels of their guns pointed in our direction.

Guns? Seriously? The Nightstalkers' tech could disarm a gun in seconds. But, I suppose they still worked against humans.

"What the hell, Marcus! You said we'd be safe here," I yelled, reaching for Sunny.

He turned and gave me a steady look I'd seen before. He had everything under control.

"Turn that Jeep around. You've got no business here," a gruff voice called across the meadow.

Marcus took a deep breath and swiped his matted hair from his eyes before he responded. "A friend told me about this place. We're here for shelter."

"There's no room," a second, distinctly female, voice spoke.

Sunny stirred in my arms. She rubbed her worn eyes and gave a wide yawn before sitting up. Looking at the armed bodies surrounding us, her body hummed with light as she let loose a wild scream. Her wail shook the birds from the trees, making them swarm like bees. As they careened overhead, a few fell dead to the ground as if shocked by Sunny's scream. When they hit the ground, I could have sworn they were smoldering. I leaned outside the Jeep and studied one of the birds that fell nearby, puzzled as to why it was burnt beyond recognition.

Shaking my head, I eased back into the seat when the gruff voice questioned, "Is that a female child?"

Before Marcus could answer, the woman asked, "How old is she?"

Marcus turned in his seat. He gave a terse nod before I answered.

"Six," I choked out. The word scratched at my throat.

The guns lowered at once. The army walked back to the cover of the woods, except for one man who strode across the dry grass toward us. When the man was ten feet away, Marcus leaned across the seat and reached for his Glock. He raised it.

"Drop your weapon," he said.

The man froze and unslung the rifle from his shoulder, lowering it slowly to the ground.

"The one from your leg holster, too," Marcus added.

Bending down, his hand grabbed at the weapon secured under camouflage material and tossed it to the side.

"You can approach now," Marcus said.

The man walked to the Jeep. Before he reached the door, he removed the scarf covering his face and the hat from his head. I gasped as a mane of long blond hair tumbled down across her shoulders.

She kept her arms raised as she spoke. "I've got no other weapons." She turned from Marcus and focused on Sunny and me. "Bet you're hungry." A slight twitch of a smile formed at the corner of her mouth. Neither of us spoke. We only stared at the woman with sparkling, green eyes.

"May, I?" she asked pointing to the passenger seat. Marcus paused for a moment.

Was that joy I saw flicker across his eyes? He must have been as shocked as me to see a woman.

"Can I get in the Jeep?" she asked, slower this time like he was brainless.

Marcus snapped out of it and reached to unlock the door. She climbed in and pointed at the gate. "Drive up through the entrance and let's see what we can do about getting you fed."

Turning the key in the ignition, Marcus turned and gave me a confident look before pulling forward. Relief washed over me as we moved to the entrance. Without Sunny we would be dead. People in the world fell into two camps now: those who saw young girls as a threat and generally shot first and asked questions later and others who knew girls needed to be protected. I was grateful these people were the latter.

The camp sat at the highest peak of the rim. Man-made shelters constructed out of scrap metal and decaying wood leaned against vast outcroppings of red stone that hung in the air like a suspended wave. People milled about the area. Some snuffed out the last gasp of a fire while others secured supplies in a far corner of the settlement. When Marcus killed the engine I held out my hand and helped Sunny from the back seat. A murmur rose from the crowd before her feet hit the ground.

The hurried camp came to a complete standstill. Each inhabitant rooted in place as if held by a mysterious force. Every eye focused on Sunny.

My protective, brotherly instinct kicked in, but Marcus got to Sunny first, shielding her from the intense gazes. Somehow he always knew when we needed protection.

The woman cleared her throat. "Please welcome our newest inhabitants. They will be staying for a while."

My eyes shifted across the crowd, waiting for it. Eventually a man with a black, braided beard stepped from the group. "They can't stay," he insisted. "Having her here is like shooting up a flare, signaling them to our location. You're placing the entire camp at risk, Lucy."

Marcus began to argue, but Lucy cut him off. "This child is like any other human. She deserves the right to feel safe. To be protected. We'll take precautions but she is staying."

The crowd grumbled and argued over Sunny's presence. I held on to her shoulders tightly and she shivered under my grasp.

When it was clear Lucy would not back down, the group dispersed and went back to their chores. It was obvious she held power in the camp and I was grateful she was on our side.

Lucy turned and winked at Sunny. "You like eggs?" Sunny slid closer to me but offered a slight nod. As Lucy strode toward the camp, Sunny squeezed my hand. I looked down at her and smiled. "Come on," I said. "I'm starving too."

Our presence upset the camp the first few days. Men and women steered clear of us when we walked through the settlement. Their eyes moved curiously over us and I knew what they were thinking. Why hadn't Marcus and I ditched Sunny sooner? It would have meant a longer life for us.

The thought never once crossed my mind but I wondered about Marcus. We slowed him down and made his life more complicated. When he saved us that night in the junkyard, we were starving and close to becoming a meal for a pack of wild dogs. From that moment on, his protection never wavered. I never quite understood his decision until I caught him staring at Sunny one night. His look a combination of loss and regret. I knew then he, too, had lost everything.

Lucy visited us frequently and always brought something to entertain us. Sometimes it was an odd piece of scrap paper and a nubby pencil to draw a picture, or a handful of dried fruit—which was a treat after eating nothing but wild game for the past few weeks.

When she and Marcus talked, I sat a few feet away and pretended not to listen. There were concerns about the coming winter and the lack of shelter. Although the desert was scorching hot during the day, once the sun went down the air turned frigid. The settlement planned to stay through September and then move down into the valley at the first sign of fall. From the changing weather, I knew that was only weeks away.

I held my breath and tried to act busy as they discussed Sunny and me.

"I think we should split up," Lucy said. "You should take Sunny higher into the mountains where she's easier to hide." Marcus shook his head in protest as Lucy continued.

"I'll take Austin down to a camp in the valley. He's thirteen. He needs to go to school and be around other boys his age," she added.

"I can't separate them," Marcus whispered. I looked up and saw them staring at me.

"Maybe we should continue this conversation another time," Lucy murmured. She stood and called her goodbyes before exiting out the cave entrance.

"I'll never agree to that plan," I hissed at Marcus. "I made my mother a promise the day the Nightstalkers arrived. Did you know their massive steel bodies and claws leveled everything on our street in minutes?" Marcus's eyes shifted to the ground unable to meet mine. "In that moment my mom knew Sunny would never make it without me."

I swallowed my anger wondering if my protests would mean anything. Adults always thought they knew better. They were wrong this time.

Marcus stepped forward and put a reassuring hand on my shoulder. "We'll work something out, Austin," he said before turning to leave.

Marcus worked alongside the settlers, forming a quick bond which surprised me. He always seemed leery of new people, but I knew Lucy had something to do with his new, relaxed state. Gone was his anxious gaze, and when Lucy appeared, the lines softened in his face. With her, he found comfort Sunny and I couldn't provide.

Sunny grew increasingly attached to Lucy. Our mother died just over a year ago and she never knew our father. Lucy was kind and instinctively knew when Sunny needed a gentle touch. Sunny still refused to speak, but Lucy managed to get her to laugh one time. Something I never managed to do in the last 442 days we were on the run. How could you laugh when twelve-foot-tall creatures with spindly legs, giant metallic heads and three-foot-long serrated teeth were hunting you?

The rising smoke from the fire brought everyone to the center of the settlement as final decisions were made for the departure.

Vehicles bulged with oversized bags that spilled out of open windows. Tires sunk deep into the red earth from the weight of their cargo. Women gathered their meager possessions while men cleaned their rifles. The pungent smell of gun cleaner clung to the air and I jumped every time a bullet clicked sharply into a weapon's chamber.

When the final flicker of sunlight disappeared from the sky, Marcus walked us to the cave that had become our home. He sat us down and in a choked whisper told us the plan. In the morning we would be moving on, separately. He felt the settlement's trip would bring too much attention to Sunny. Instead, the three of us would move west trying to escape the cold.

I shook his hand and he smiled before securing me in a brisk hug. "Thanks for sticking with us... and keeping us together," I said in a tight voice.

"You're my family now," he said pulling back, his gaze shifting between Sunny and me. The thin hairs of his graying mustache quivered as he spoke.

He secured our dark pit for the last time. In the cave the hole was shallower. We weren't in the open and Sunny's energy could be slightly hidden by the deep rock surrounding us.

I watched as his muscles twitched with the movement of soil. I prayed I would be able to dig that quickly one day.

At dawn, I woke to Sunny's pulsing glow. I reached for her shoulder to wake her, when I heard voices shoot down the air tube.

"We just heard from them," Lucy's voice shook with excitement. "Forces will be here within the hour. They've promised our safety in return for the girl."

"Quiet. You'll wake them," Marcus growled.

Tiny pricks of ice crept up my spine, and even though Sunny radiated enough heat to melt ice cubes, my entire body was cold. My fists tightened at my side. I slammed my eyes shut and covered my mouth, smothering the building fury threatening to rip from my lungs.

When Marcus pulled us from the earth a while later, I plastered a smile to my face. He gave me a wide, traitorous grin before leaving to grab us breakfast.

In a panic, I grabbed our bags and started packing every item within reach. Flipping through Marcus's satchel, I spied his Glock and slid it into my bag. Holding Sunny's hand, I pulled her out along the thick woods behind the cave. Pressing a finger to my lips, I urged her to keep quiet.

Whipping her head around frantically she motioned over and over to the camp. I dragged her a hundred yards into the forest and pulled her against the base of a Ponderosa pine. "Sunny, listen. Lucy and Marcus are going to hand you over to the Nightstalkers." Her lip trembled. "We need to move deeper into the woods, away from the settlement. Somewhere they can't find us." Tears streamed down her face as a quiet sob escaped her throat.

"I know you're afraid, but I can take care of us. I promise." I knew I was the only one who could protect us now. We needed to disappear fast or we wouldn't live through the day.

Sunny's breathing turned ragged and I pulled her into a fierce hug. Her body shook uncontrollably. I realized then that it wasn't fear shaking my sister's body but the pulse of the ground beneath our feet. The movement shook the pine needles from the trees until they rained down in a heavy, green mist. The once quiet forest careened with the sound of moving gears and motors.

Sunny's face froze in a mask of terror. An army of Nightstalkers was near. Before I could move, heavy footsteps pounded through the forest as echoing voices burst off the trees. Marcus's yell cut through the noise first as he stopped twenty feet in front of us.

"Austin, what the hell are you doing?" he said in a strangled whisper.

The lines around his eyes deepened and his mouth set in a thin line. He approached me, the barrel of his weapon pointed directly at my head. He released a high-pitched whistle that hung on the wind and reinforcements descended from treetops and emerged from camouflaged barriers set up all along the forest floor. They marched toward us. Their weapons pointed at their targets: Sunny and me.

"You sold us out," I snarled.

Marcus stepped closer and latched the safety of his weapon in place with a sharp click. His eyes never left my face.

"You can lower your weapons. They're not going anywhere," he called to the group who slowly holstered their guns.

Marcus shrugged his shoulders and released a pitying sigh. "Sorry, Austin. I had to earn your trust. That took a while. Then, when I knew you were ready, I goaded you and Sunny along. The camp's been waiting a long time for her."

"Why would you do this?" I asked.

He shook his head, an almost sad look covering his face. "It's all about survival, my boy. We give them Sunny and they let us live peacefully." His eyes shifted to the ground. He knew his choice was all kinds of wrong. "One little girl for the entire group's safety. It was a choice I had to make."

"We won't go easy," I growled. "I'm not some clueless kid."

Without hesitating, I pulled out the Glock and fired. The bullet rammed into his chest and he flailed back, landing in a pile of decaying leaves.

The settlers rushed us in a solid line, Lucy in the lead. She had a crazed, almost feral look covering her face. They would not shoot until they were closer. If Sunny died so would all their plans.

"You're outnumbered," Lucy said taking tentative steps toward me. Her long braid swung behind her. The determined look in her eyes told me she would do anything to take Sunny. How had I been so easily fooled?

The Nightstalkers entered the clearing, their sharp claws taking down nearby trees in one swift motion. Their steel heads bobbed up and down. An angry, keening noise shot from the lead beast's mouth.

My feet shuffled back along the fallen pine needles as I pushed Sunny around the tree. A second later the first round released and I dove for cover. The bullet zinged past my ear and exploded into a tree directly behind us. I scrambled around and crouched next to Sunny.

The ground still hummed and pulsed with the sound of grinding gears, as the Nightstalkers drew closer. I imagined them securing Sunny in their thick metallic arms before they swung her up into their airtight pods, drooling over the power pulsing within her.

Additional gunfire came in quick bursts. Ricocheting bullets sent bark flying into the air. My heart pounded as I formulated a plan. It was a short distance to a bank of trees. If we could get there we'd be out of the line of fire.

I secured the gun between my sweaty hands. My body pulsed with adrenaline. I readied my body to spring. Sunny's trembling hands grabbed at me. She shook me hard trying to get my attention.

Tears filled her eyes as I watched the light grow inside her. A halo of gold encompassed her entire body bathing us both in warm light. As she moved, the light flickered and singed the ground around her. Smoke rose around us and clouded my vision. Her fingers throbbed with emanating heat and slipped from my grasp as she rounded the tree.

I grabbed at her trying to pull her back. The tattered fabric of her skirt slipped through my fingers and she was gone.

A scream ripped from my throat. I stood to chase her, but the rumble of the Nightstalkers pounding against the earth knocked me off balance.

Before I could take a step, a surge of heat grabbed at me. I crawled behind the tree as what felt like a writhing flame enveloped my body. Gasping, but unable to take in any air, I curled into a ball trying to escape the churning fire clawing at my head. It coursed down my body before releasing at my fingertips.

The scent of charred wood and melting metal tore at my nose. I hunched lower, afraid the heat would engulf my entire face. As the flames continued to lick my skin, agonizing screams filled the air. I said a final prayer, waiting for death.

But just as quickly as the heat came, it disappeared. Opening my eyes, I expected to find my skin charred black, but it was still its normal color. Somehow the trunk of the tree had protected me from the penetrating blaze.

I sat in stunned silence looking at my untouched body before grief swallowed me. Tears spilled from my eyes in long streams. I'd made one promise—one I hadn't been able to keep. I thought about Sunny in the hands of the Nightstalkers and fury quickly squashed my sadness.

I readied myself to step around the tree. I would fire the remaining bullets in the Glock, knowing death would be better than becoming a slave to the Nightstalkers. I refused to spend the rest of my life working in the dark pit of the mines, forced to search for alternate sources of energy beyond our planet's female children. Death would be a gift compared to that future.

I placed my hand on the Glock's trigger. I set my feet. My heart pounded in my chest. Then I heard it. A sweet lilting voice singing just above a whisper. I stayed silent. My sister was gone. The only thing left of her was an imaginary hum on the wind.

I moved around the tree. My body thrummed with adrenaline and fear. The Glock tightened in my hands. The forest was cloaked in thin gray mist. Piles of smoldering ash lay where the settlers once stood. Smoke rose from their incinerated bodies. Dark tendrils glided up through the treetops.

The smell of charred flesh twisted my insides. I turned and looked for the army of Nightstalkers. The forest was empty except for more piles of ash. A low burning flame encircled a single serrated tooth near my foot.

Falling to my knees, I cursed and pounded the ground until my fists were numb. I screamed at the treetops wondering how I would survive in this wasteland without my sister.

As my head bent forward and sank into the ash, the song hummed in my ears again. I raised my eyes. I blinked several times before I saw her—Sunny walking toward me—completely untouched. Her hair bounced along her shoulders and her smile grew wide as she reached me. I pulled her into my arms and watched as her glow flickered like a fading candle reaching the end of its wick. The sound of her voice, which had been absent too long, reassured me the moment was real.

Her eyes held mine in a steady gaze and in that moment I understood her power. Her building energy was a potent force that not only powered the Nightstalkers, but could also incinerate everything in her wake. She, and others like her, would be the key to the Nightstalkers destruction.

I swung her around into a piggyback and walked through the silence of the forest. We were on our own again. But we were together. As we crunched through the scattered bits of metal strewn across the ground, she leaned forward and sang quietly in my ear, the song of protest and survival.

"Three Blind Mice. Three Blind Mice."

LITTLE LEAGUE

Cat Woods

TOP OF THE SECOND.
Devils: seven.
Saints: zero.

If Little League had bouncers they would have recognized the unsettled look of Spectator Five and removed him from the stands before the first pitch. As it was, he went unnoticed in his baseball cap, team jersey, and grandfatherly beard. Oh sure, he got loud. They all did. Cheering on their players with "just one more strike, Pitch," or consoling others with an, "It's okay, Batter. You'll get it next time."

That's the nature of Little League baseball.

Sweaty moms wiping grit from their eyes while their pint-sized babes swung at mispitched balls. Pacing dads calling reminders for greater concentration or quicker hands. Escalating as always, as the game wore on and the gap widened between the teams.

It was just the thing Coach D loved.

He loved the dirt and the grime. He loved the way the sun beat down relentlessly on the field and made everyone just a bit short-tempered. Especially Spectator Five.

"Come on, Pitch. Just throw 'em another strike. He ain't gonna swing anyways." And the louder Five got, the more bold others became. Soon the Devils themselves joined in, shouting phrases too sharp and inappropriate for such young mouths.

Inevitably, this agitated the Saints' fans. They grumbled at the poor sportsmanship exhibited by the opposing team and shifted their focus away from the game and onto the spectators.

The Saints floundered under the pressure, striking out in rapid succession and letting another five runs come in.

Bottom of the third.

Score: twelve-zero. Three more runs for the Devils and the Saints faced a mercy-rule loss.

The Devils' dugout echoed with victory cheers. They billowed out on a sudden gust of wind and blew into the Saints' dugout where calm kids surrounded their crouching coach. The huddle broke and the nine Saints hustled to their positions on field.

A cooling breeze rippled through the crowd and ruffled the pitcher's hair. He adjusted his cap and warmed up. His pitch was straight and true. A meatball easily hit, and the bases filled up with red-suited runners. One homerun and the game would end sixteen-zero, effectively ending the Saints' season, and leaving the Devils open for a shot at the championship game.

By some minor miracle, the Saints held firm, catching an impossible pop fly and tagging out a Devil too quick off the bag for his own good. Two outs.

Coach D slammed his stat book to the ground and stomped on it. "What in Hell were you thinking? We had 'em. All you had to do was stay on base."

The Devil ran past, head down under the coach's wrath.

The outburst spurred on the Saints' fans who turned their frustration on the ump. "Hey, Blue, you can't let him talk to his kids like that."

On the other side of the chain link fence, Peter tugged down his mask and waved the next batter forward. "I'm not here to judge, just to count the strikes against them."

The Saints' pitcher wound up. The strike landed in the catcher's mitt with a resounding thud. Above the cheering, Five's voice rang out. "You better swing next time. No grandson of mine will strike out looking."

The catcher tossed the ball back.

Another strike whizzed past the Devil at bat.

The fans erupted, their cheers mingling to create a single voice. "One more, Pitch. One more. You can do it. Just play catch."

"Strike out now and you'll be sittin' the bench." Coach D yelled.

Another murmur washed over the Saints' fans, this time in support of the batter. Clouds scuttled in, darkening the field. In the distance, thunder rumbled.

The crowd quieted as the pitch sailed in high and the batter took a half-swing—stopping just in time—and looked to the ump.

Peter clicked his counter. "Ball one."

Spectator Five leaned forward and spit a stream of sunflower seeds to the ground. "Don't you be swingin' at that junk."

Two more balls bounced on home plate before finding the catcher's glove. Balls by Peter's count. And still, Coach D shouted, rivaling Spectator Five in volume and condescension.

The batter's shoulders sagged and tears shimmered in his eyes.

Peter touched his hands over his head. "Full count!"

A pitch and a miss.

"Strike three!" Peter signaled to the Devils' dugout with an outstretched arm. "You're out!"

Avoiding his grandfather's gaze, the batter stomped back to the dugout, threw his helmet to the ground and smashed his bat into the dirt.

Top of the fourth brought the possible implementation of the ten-run mercy rule. The Saints needed three runs to stay alive.

As the Devils' pitcher warmed up, the temperature dropped. Sprinkles plopped into the dust around the stands. Smoke filled the air as the burgers at the concession stand sizzled and burned. Through the haze, the practice pitches crossed the plate, hard and fast. No meatball pitches to help the bottom of the Saints' batting order. The crowd sighed in resignation at the impending one-two-three. Several fans stood and started packing their lawn chairs and sunflower seeds in anticipation of the game's end.

"Batter's up."

Saints' Batter Eight took the plate.

Pitch.

Thud.

"Stee-rike one!"

"It's okay, Batter. The next one's yours."

Pitch.

Thud.

"Stee-rike two.

"Now you've seen it. You know what to do."

Spectator Five doffed his hat, his hair sticking up in two spikey curls over each temple. "He's yours, Pitcher. He don't even swing. Probly couldn't hit it even if he did."

Coach D grinned from the dugout.

As thunder rumbled ever closer, the Saints' fans rallied. Their voices rang out over the wind-swept field. "The next one's yours."

Pitch, swing, crack.

The ball soared over the second baseman.

Another batter, another base.

The Saints' score eased upward.

Top of the sixth.

Saints leading, seventeen-twelve.

Saints: two outs, bases loaded.

Batter Four stepped to the plate. He lifted his bat and nodded skyward, closed his eyes and settled in.

The pitch came in low. A swing and a miss.

A second strike followed.

The Saints' Coach called from the third base line. "Keep your head in the game. Don't chase the wrong ball and wait for your pitch."

On the bated breath of the fans, Batter Four waited through three balls, his body jumping as the pitch thudded in the catcher's mitt.

The Devil released his pitch, straight and true. Batter Four swung hard and cranked it down the base line. He rounded first, then second. On third Coach waved him in.

The right fielder threw to the second baseman who gunned it home.

Ball against runner.

"Slide. Slide. SLIDE!"

Despite the chants, Batter Four ran on.

The catcher stretched his arm high and the ball smacked into his glove. He swung it down. Step. Step. Tag.

Bag. The runner miscalculated his last step and brought his foot down on the edge of home plate. His ankle rolled and a loud crack reverberated through the air.

He dropped to the ground, screaming and clutching his ankle.

"He's out." Spectator Five flew off the bench and rattled the fence between him and the field. "Call him out."

Peter dismissed him with a wave and attended the runner, whose ankle canted awkwardly to the side.

"He's out. He's out. Out. Out. OUT!"

Spectator Five led the new chant. Thunder crackled and bloated clouds threatened to open wide, the weather as foul as Five's mouth.

A brave mom stood up and faced her crowd. "A child is hurt and all you can think about is winning. You should be ashamed of yourselves."

Immediately, a quiet settled over the stands.

Peter knelt over the runner and tried to calm him. "Why didn't you slide?"

Batter Four smiled through his tears. "I wanted to get a homerun."

The Saints' coach tousled the boy's hair. "Well, you got home, but I don't know if you got the run."

Peter cleaned the base and reluctantly called his decision. "Out."

The sun peeked out behind the clouds, its rays shining on the scoreboard.

Twenty-twelve, Saints leading.

The Devils struck out one by one, and the game ended to the sobbing of Spectator Five.

The same mom shook her head in disgust. "Losing isn't the end of the world."

The ump nodded toward the Saints' coach. He stood on the field with his chin tilted toward the score board. His face seemed to shimmer in the midday sun, his attire as crisp and white as if he'd just pulled it from the washer. "It is today."

REBIRTH

A.M. Supinger

SELKIES ARE NOT BORN, NOR are they made from magic and spells. Pain is the only way for a seal to shed its skin and walk among humans. To emerge from the sea is to emerge from one's self—and that, it could be said, is a kind of magic.

Geraldine had always been amazed with the tales of shifters and the people they lived amidst.

The cliffs and sand were appealing because they were mostly unexplored by her kind. People moved about on limbs that carried them upright, and they all looked happy. Smiles stretched their wide, hairless faces most of the time. Only once had tears greeted Geraldine.

Long ago, before she knew what tears were, the woman's sobs had torn at her heart. The emotions were powerful, churning the very waters with grief. Nothing had been so sad since, and Geraldine wanted *that*.

Oh, she wanted to smile and dance, too, but the pain and anguish were intriguing in some dark way. What was it like, she wondered, to feel that deeply? To care about something that much?

She would soon know. Escaping from home for a few hours was easy—her family expected her to do that every now and then. But time enough to gather the courage needed to change? That was something entirely different.

The pain was what kept most seals tethered to the sea; ripping free of her flippers would hurt past endurance. But she could do it. Others had... Ondine, Roanine. They had married human lovers before the call of the ocean melted their resolve. But Geraldine didn't want to marry and live forever on land. She only wanted to be free to explore the unknown.

So, when the tide brought her to a secluded beach, she crawled up onto the scorching sand. Every shard of the crushed shells littering the shore ripped at her tender, fur-covered flesh. The smooth rocks near her underwater home never tore at her this way... but then again, seals weren't meant to wallow on man's land.

Using only her front flippers, Geraldine dug into the rough sand. When her body was half buried, she closed her eyes. Took one breath.

Two.

Three.

Four.

Five.

Then she exhaled, letting her fear go. Five seconds was all she allowed herself now. She'd done her thinking before, back in the balmy waves, where her friends and family swam about their business, unaware of her morbid curiosity.

Pushing up, arching her back, she thought of rebirth. As a pup, like all pups, she'd been told about the process. Old

Homin's great grandmother was friends with Ondine, and her infamous tale had been passed down once she'd returned to the sea. *Think of rebirth,* Old Homin had said. *Imagine peeling away the salt water and drying out in the sun. Your fur will oblige, as long as you're willing to pay the price.*

Imagining herself without fur was hard—she only had a few glimpses of human women to go on. But picturing herself dry was not hard; she'd tried that before. Only days after Old Homin had shared his tale, Geraldine had gone up to a beach and perched on a rock. Knowing it was foolish—that she could be caught by sharks or people—hadn't stopped her.

Nor did it stop her now.

Her snout went up, eyes wide open, and she stared into the orange ball that lit the human world. A tingling pull started at the juncture where her gums met her teeth, where soft and hard had always before worked in harmony to keep her alive. The tingle turned ominous as she visualized crawling free of a pile of fur, her pale limbs bare to the hot sun.

Pain seared her jaw and inched down her throat. Every hair stood on end, each alive with a strange, wrenching awareness.

It was happening.

An intense wave of heat swept through her body, and steam curled out of her nostrils. She huffed out hard breaths, her lungs pumping ash instead of air. Keeping the image of humanity in her mind was hard when she felt like she was dying, but never did she waver.

When her flippers cracked open and her blood poured out onto the broken shells around her, Geraldine almost panicked. Almost. But the crimson was brighter than the sun. *Stronger* than the sun. It held her gaze like the orb in the sky never could. Her life was draining away, and it fascinated her.

It hurt, and the pain spread faster now, but her mind kept the rebirth firmly anchored. Only… now her skin was red instead of white. When she moved, her limbs didn't gracefully sway the way she'd imagined she'd walk. Now she could only see a wretch who flopped helplessly around in the sand, trapped in a body that would never work, limbs twisted and deformed.

Frightened, Geraldine slammed her eyelids shut and tried to breathe. But her lungs were still on fire. Her body was cracking open. Her blood was seeping into the shore. Whether she wanted to or not, she was probably going to die. Rebirth would end in death.

When the bloody image of her crippled human form finally faded from her mind, Geraldine shuddered.

The physical pain had been excruciating… but the anguish of seeing herself stranded, alone—trapped—had been the true torture. Freedom to move, to explore, was the one part of herself she couldn't give up. Ever. Not even to walk upright or cry human tears.

Geraldine let out a shaky breath, wincing when her tender lungs protested.

The pain, it seemed, wouldn't fade with her failure. Perhaps it would stay with her always, a reminder of her inability to let go.

She was fine with that. As much as she'd wanted to change— as *long* as she'd wanted to change—it had never occurred to her that she would fail. Not once.

Humility might be her lesson, pain her reminder, she thought.

But when she huffed out a sour laugh, it didn't sound right. It sounded… human.

Geraldine jerked her head up and blinked away the sandy tears gluing her eyes shut. It hurt—but not nearly enough to distract her. Nothing could have. Her eyes scanned the pale mess before her, unbelieving and horrified.

A joke, she thought. It is a cruel joke. This can't happen.

Her body wasn't seal, and it wasn't human. Not even the red-skinned cripple she'd been so frightened of. Instead, she was both. Her front flippers—or what had been her front flippers—were cracked open around pale human arms, which were attached to the sides of a pale human chest. But below the navel, where legs should have sprouted, was a red tail. Her normal tail was gone, replaced by a broken, shriveled lump that couldn't possibly swim through water. Deformed. Hideous. Twisted.

Bloody, just like in her mind. Except now she was half herself and half something else. A bit of what she used to be—a bit of what she could have been.

Tears and screams tore her smoke-ravaged throat as Old Homin's voice whispered through her mind: *Only those who can give themselves entirely up can make the change. If you can't leave yourself behind, you won't survive. After all, a seal can't live on land. Only a selkie can.*

Geraldine sobbed into the blood-drenched sand, fear and anger battling inside her. She'd done this to herself—ruined herself. She'd die this way, broken like the shells crushed beneath her, left to rot on a beach like a wayward jellyfish. No one would look for her here. No one would find her.

She'd fade anonymously, waste into sea foam.

Her tears stormed through the air, rattling the peace of the shore and riling the very waves. She screamed again, uncaring that grief had found her at last, hating the wrenching near her heart. It didn't fascinate her now, when her existence was nigh but a blink from ending. She'd die and never get to share this discovery, this newly explored tragedy—the horror of her rebirth.

When the sorrow-laden waves washed up on her, choking her human lungs, she didn't fight. The salty taste of her home swept her off the sand, out of her shell hole. The ragged bits of her sealskin sank while her deformed body drifted… drifted….

CRUMBS

Jean Oram

S CANNING THE NEIGHBORHOOD through my viewfinder, I finally spied the man I was waiting for. Etched into his urban wear was a layer of grime that camouflaged with the blackened rubble, torn earth, and heaved streets. For hours I had ruthlessly beat away the splinter of hope that kept slipping under my skin. At every mental turn I shut out the thought of what I might have to do to guarantee my own survival, if and when he returned.

And now here he was.

He had returned to his demolished split-level, looking beaten down around the edges, but still as dangerously handsome as the day I moved in across the street. And still acting as though I failed to exist.

Maybe he hadn't seen me.

Silently I worked my way down the charred hood of my neighbor's destroyed Plymouth, and perched on the corner of the cool, pockmarked metal. Feet on the bumper, I propped my elbows on my knees to help steady the heavy, metal device I aimed at Ed's skull.

I scrutinized his scavenging movements to determine whether he was friend or foe. The war had changed people. Changed me. I lightly touched my fingertips to the stained knife resting on the hood to assure myself of its readiness.

I had a clear shot between the melted and twisted form that used to be my Yaris and the overturned enemy tank. I thumbed the zoom button on my Canon EOS 5D to zero in on Ed's face, hoping to gather intel from his expression.

Nothing. I lowered the camera a notch and peeked over it for the crispness of real life. Too far away.

I hid behind the camera again, relieved by the façade of being masked despite knowing my filthy jeans, sooty shirt, and tumbleweed hair helped me blend in.

Ed poked through charred rubble, nudging at tattered and destroyed possessions with the toe of his loafer, coughing as he disturbed layers of ash. I acted like I was taking shot after shot, framing and reframing, fooling myself into believing that my boss, who in all likelihood was no longer alive, would finally be swayed into giving me the promotion I longed for.

My shots were full of humanity and struggle. Emotion. Aftermath. They told a story and were worthy of an exclusive: The flash war that all but destroyed the world's population in eleven days.

These pictures would put me on the world's photojournalist stage. My talent recognized.

Sadness pulled at my core: fleetingly I allowed reality to bully her way in, her talons dragging me further into a frightening abyss.

If I had batteries.

Or a job. A boss. A computer. A newspaper or magazine to

publish my shots. The chances were slim that any of these things still existed. Sure, rumors swirled among the few remaining souls. Rumors of pockets containing unaffected life. Food. Shelter. Safety.

Some said north. Some said islands in the Pacific. Others said bunkers in the mountains. But they were just that—rumors. Rumors that weighted my heart like concrete shoes. Rumors of the unattainable, and much too distant to help me.

Unattainable and distant like Ed. I jerked my finger on the shutter button and caught Ed cautiously sniffing a blackened can. His search for food was no better than my own futile quests. Plus, little did he know, a band of not-so-merry men had already scavenged all the food on our street. The only useful item I'd managed to find was a bent kitchen knife—the one that had already come in handy for turning away unwanted attention and a pushy chorus of guys. I touched the blade again and flicked a glance over my shoulder. A crater backed by a mound of smoking, vacant rubble. Nothing. Nobody.

I was getting paranoid.

I returned my focus to Ed, jaw tight.

"Look at me," I whispered. "Show me the whites of your eyes."

I waited for him to turn around so I could see who he'd become.

And for him to see me. To see who I'd always been.

He turned away to inspect the smoldering wreckage in his backyard. The remains of a rebuilt Ford Fairlane.

I let out a quiet harrumph. Ignored. Over a car.

Sighing, I shifted to return circulation to my tingling left foot.

Always unseen by the ones I desired most. Crumbs of their attention left me starving while I turned back a feast offered by creeps. I took a deep breath to ease the tension in my shoulders.

I snapped a poorly framed shot that cut off Ed's head and right arm. The camera grew steadily heavier, similar to the reality that surrounded me. Watching the end of the Eleven Day War was surreal. The two sides, waking up to the fact that there was nothing left to fight over but mass destruction, stopped suddenly as if commanded by an unseen force. They straightened, peered around as though the sun hurt their eyes, and walked away from what was left of their artillery.

The look of stunned horror at what they had accomplished would haunt me for my remaining days. One soldier shot himself under the streetlight where, high above, the provincial premier hung limp and deflated. I blinked back tears, knowing I had captured every one of my raw emotions in digital. I didn't need to deal with it. It was sealed in the black box with Canon stamped on it.

Later, I told myself. Later. When you are safe.

Hunger chewed at my stomach and my attention turned back to Ed.

Hardly good eats.

I gave myself a shake. I wasn't built for this kind of world.

Ed moved to the edge of my view between the car and tank, and I carefully shimmied my way back up the hood to keep him in my line of sight. Shoulders slumped, he jangled the empty shelves of a crumpled mini-fridge.

Everything good has already been scavenged, Ed. Come to me. Look up... look up.

A raindrop plinked on my hand and, instinctively, I pulled my windbreaker up to shield my camera, my eye never straying from the viewfinder.

Ed bent over to peer into the fridge and my finger landed hard on the shutter button. My lips curved into a shy smile before falling in disappointment.

No batteries. After all those years of gardening in the front yard, waiting for him to come home and give his customary nod before entering his house. Naïve enough to hope for a "hello," or possibly even a lonely gal's money shot—a good gander at his lovely, runner's buttocks as he bent over to retrieve the newspaper left on his step. Or even more fantasy-like, for him to shake out the paper, see my photo credit on the front page and hurry across the street to pay his long-overdue compliments on my garden, my photos, and my witty, newly discovered sense of humor. Then he would whisk me into his house, and we would never be parted.

I blinked and lowered my camera. What was the point of rehashing fantasies? I was still invisible and now I needed him even more—for an entirely different kind of single girl's survival.

The stench of rotting flowers wafted from the massive crater behind me. God, I'd always hated flowers. And yet I had cried great, fat tears of anguish over their destruction. How stupid was that?

I shifted so I couldn't see the blackness where my gardens used to be and continued to keep tabs on Ed's futile search.

Why couldn't I yell out "hello?" Why hide behind my camera? Even now with the flash war and homelessness in common I couldn't force myself to draw his attention.

The stray rain cloud moved on, the sprinkle of cool drops waning. I shrugged out of my jacket, keeping an eye on Ed, the only sign of friendly life on our block for the past seven and a half hours. Riffling through my massive camera bag/purse I pushed aside the empty mace canister and dug out a package of crushed Premium Plus crackers I'd pilfered from Subway less than fourteen days ago. Only two weeks ago I was standing in the brightly lit restaurant, the planet still at peace, and debating olives over peppers. The rumbling in my stomach made me wish I had opted for both, even if for a sliver of extra body fat to help carry me through this decimated land.

Carefully, I poured half the crumbs into my mouth and considered the pros and cons of eating the rest now instead of later. The crackers tickled the back of my throat and I hacked into my hand, trying not to lose any crumbs. Ed straightened at the noise, turned his cloudy blue eyes towards me, and gave his familiar, customary head nod that made my heart do an awkward little jolt followed by a backflip.

I used to wish he'd acknowledge me so I wouldn't be alone while all my friends married. His strong arms around me in the night, holding me close, staving off the loneliness that would grip me like a python seeking dinner. Now, I craved his acknowledgement to prove I'd survived. His strong arms and presence to stave off the loneliness of starving alone.

I needed him now for an entirely different kind of safety in numbers.

Cheeks warm, I lifted my hand to wave. I gave him a trembling half smile.

"Hi," I said loud enough for him to hear. "My name is Anastasia—Ana. Would you like some crumbs?"

THE LAST PERFORMANCE OF THE NEIGHBORHOOD SUMMER THEATRE FESTIVAL

R.S. Mellette

IT WAS A NICE NIGHT. THERE WERE no stars. Henry could not remember there ever being stars, but he'd seen them on TV.

He remembered pointing to the screen while watching E.T. as a child. "What are those?" he asked his mother.

"Those are stars," she said.

"Where are they?"

"In the sky, silly."

"In whose sky?"

"Our sky. *The* sky. What other sky is there?"

Henry looked at the sky. It was a nice night, cool after the first hot day of the season. It was clear, but there were no stars. All he could see were streetlights, security lights, and architectural lighting. They lit up the horizon above the trees and buildings with fluorescence, neon, and Magnesium-Halogen. He was older now. His mother was gone. He had everything a man could want in life, but still hadn't seen the stars.

Walking at night was not done in Henry's neighborhood. Oh, it was safe. It was a nice neighborhood. Private security patrols and cameras watched every house to make sure it stayed that way. Sprinklers made sure the lawns stayed green under the blistering sun. More beautiful homes could not be found in the city, but no one walked unless they had to.

Not many people know their neighbors anymore, thought Henry. I wonder if they ever did.

Standing in his driveway, hands in pockets, Henry was aware of his home behind him. It held all the stuff he'd accumulated in his fifty years, and yet that night it felt empty. He had every *thing* a man could want, and he wondered if it was human nature that made him want a something more. Something else.

He began to walk.

It wasn't long before he'd left his affluent neighborhood to find himself strolling past well-lit homes and apartments, each filled with families watching separate shows, on separate devices, in separate rooms. Small businesses skirted on the edge of these domiciles. That was where Henry came across a handful of people in front of a dark, windowless building.

"Are you here for the show?"

The question came from one of the group. They were not waiting to go in. The door was open. There was no line. Nor were they on their way out. They just stood, about ten or twelve of them, kicking the dirt, mumbling under their breath, and generally looking for direction.

"I beg your pardon?" Henry did not expect to be spoken to.

"Are you here for the show?" He was an angry young man with a not-so-threatening chip on his shoulder. "'Cause if you are, you aren't."

"I'm sorry?"

"No, we're the ones who are sorry."

"He means," interrupted a young woman from the group. She seemed kinder than the man, though no less melancholy. "There isn't going to be a show."

"Oh," said Henry. "I didn't know that."

"Of course you didn't know that." It was the angry one again. "We just canceled it a few minutes ago."

"No, I didn't know there was going to be a show in the first place."

"Great," sighed another from the troupe, "one guy turns up and he doesn't even know there's a show."

Henry studied their faces by the shadowy night lights. Most were too young to be so tired and sad. The sparks of their youth were falling on cold stone.

"What kind of show is it?" Henry asked. "I don't see any cameras."

A ripple of impatience went through the group. "There are no cameras," explained a girl of long hair and patience. "This is live theatre."

"Live?"

"Yes."

Then another, "Haven't you ever seen a live play?"

Henry thought for a moment. "No. I haven't."

"Never?"

"Not that I can remember."

The group suddenly found him fascinating.

"Wow."

"Not even in school?"

Henry got defensive. "We *read* plays in school."

"They weren't meant to be read," said the patient girl.

"I think I remember watching them on video."

The angry young man stepped forward. "That was TV, Jack. We're talking theatre here."

Henry had earned his wealth by listening and learning. He dropped his defensiveness and stepped outside of himself. What a curiosity they were to each other, he and this group. Neither had seen anything like the other before.

"In fact," said Henry, "no one I know has ever been to a live theatre performance."

As the words came out of his mouth, he could tell it was a hard pill for the group to swallow. Their excitement waned. They had not found an exception to society. They had not found a freak to ridicule or even to teach. They were the strange ones. They were the freaks. They were the ones who needed to learn that the world had changed around them. Their ancient art — older than civilization itself – was dying. Was dead.

Henry sensed their despair. "What play are you doing?"

"A Mid-Summer Night's Dream."

"Really? I've heard of that one."

"Good." They were less than enthused.

"It's been done before, hasn't it?"

"Yeah," said one.

"It's Shakespeare," said another.

Of course, Henry knew who he was. "Oh, did he write that one, too?"

The patient girl stepped forward. "Look. It's been nice talking to you—"

"I'd like to see it."

"Not tonight," said the angry young man.

"When, then?"

The majority of the company looked to the angry young man, the patient girl, and an older man who had said nothing so far. "Maybe never," said the angry one. "You may never get to see this play, or any other play for that matter."

The patient girl, continued for him. "We're the last theatre company in town. Our subscribers are mostly our friends and families. We're supposed to run all summer, but without subscriptions or advanced sales, we'll have to close."

"How much longer can you stay open?"

The company's ears perked. The girl couldn't bring herself to say the words. She looked to the old man. "Not another day," he said.

There were no tears, no surprise, only bowed heads as if in prayer.

"I'm sorry to hear that," said Henry.

"Not half as sorry as we are," said the old man. "Good night."

"Good night." But Henry didn't move. The company of actors passed around him toward their cars. "I'd really like to see this show."

"And we'd like to show it to you," said the young man, "but we can't."

"Why not?"

"Besides the fact that it's no fun to perform for one person, we can't afford it."

"How much?" Henry was surprised he even asked the question, and didn't know what he would say to the answer.

The old man spoke. "Each show costs $750. That covers theatre rental, power bills, and paying the actors."

"Which hasn't happened – ever," said the girl who was once patient.

Henry thought of his house full of things, and his life only half full of experiences. "I'll tell you what," he pulled out his credit card, "if you perform this show for me tonight, I'll pay your debts, plus running expenses through the end of the week."

The look on their faces when Henry Chamberlain's card cleared was worth the money he'd spent. The show itself was icing on the cake. The actors, when not on stage, crept into the audience to spy on their fellows in scenes they hadn't watched since rehearsal.

They also watched Henry. He grinned from ear-to-ear, and laughed like Santa Claus. Occasionally, he would catch the eye of an actor in the wings staring out at him. He would wink. The actor would smile. Henry couldn't help but think how they looked like excited kids, or wood nymphs sneaking a peek through the trees at the stranger in their midst. They had made him a kid again. Halfway through the performance, he realized his face was sore from smiling.

That night, Henry had the time of his life, for he had finally seen the stars.

Bone Dust

P.S. Carrillo

ALONG THE TRAIL TO THE FORGOTTEN town of Beggars Gulch, Sophie kicked the dust off her boots watching small clouds dissipate into the warm air. The train had left her stranded without a stagecoach for hire. The stuffed saddlebags had proven too heavy and the last stretch of her journey had been spent leading her horse through the heat for nearly five miles. She stopped momentarily to check the distance traveled on the copper monitor fastened to her leather belt. The metal dial shone intensely in the sunlight. Small numbers rolled over themselves and settled on a distance informing her that one mile remained.

The letter that prompted the hard journey described the mining town as vacated but filled with promise. It also gave the details of the latest wave of Plague that had swept through the western part of the country leaving thousands dead and thousands more in a desperate state of departure and mourning.

It was widely believed that the mysterious disease had begun in the South Seas then continued east over the western territories after the complete annihilation of San Francisco. It was also considered the worst outbreak of contagion humanity had ever endured. No treatment had been found that could treat the horrific symptoms of violent stomach pains and bloody fluids that oozed from every orifice of the body. Death was nearly guaranteed and often proved to be a welcome relief for its victims.

The relentless summer sun beat down upon Sophie. She wiped the sweat from her upper lip with the back of her hand then reached to loosen her long, blond hair from a leather tie. Her thoughts drifted to the remembrance of his strong hands running through her hair as he kissed her. She felt disheveled, but would have to present herself in plain trousers and a duster coat made dustier with the travel on foot. Her thoughts drifted again to their last farewell. She would have promised him anything in that moment of passion. Traveling alone in the desert, exhausted and near collapse, Sophie pressed on, urged by the anticipation of seeing her beloved once more.

The terrain changed as Sophie came into view of the town. It was situated along a sunken hillside of the eastern Sierra Nevada mountain range. Small pine trees dotted the landscape and ramshackle structures were tucked into the dirt with no one to claim residence. A church, which had been constructed outside town weeks prior to the outbreak, could be seen in the distance, newly painted in white with its high steeple pointing to Heaven. Beside the church grounds a wooden fence enclosed a large plot of land. Simple markers identified the numerous graves of the recently departed giving the empty town a more complete sense of abandonment. Amid the desolation, even the souls of the dead seemed absent with only their bones left to fill the ground.

Sophie traveled along the fence line of the cemetery, her eyes roaming over the graves. The sun had baked and sealed the earthen tombs while small, resilient weeds had grown over the dirt. One grave appeared recently created and was elevated above the rest. A wooden cross still held the vivid colors used to identify the body below: "Vivian Olmstead, 1866-1880, Beloved Daughter." The wind had been blowing slightly and as Sophie focused on the grave marker a sudden gush of air encircled her making a whistling sound. A faint shrill cry formed on the wind, startling her. The sound was distinctly human and anguish resonated.

The wind ceased and Sophie thought of youth cruelly robbed of life. She offered a quick prayer to the dead girl then gave a quick pat to her horse's hindquarters urging it to move on. She had encountered far too many gravesites and cemeteries to be frightened.

The town's main street was lined by two rows of wooden buildings that varied in height. The construction had begun hastily when the news of gold spread across the country that Beggars Gulch was the latest camp to strike it rich. The town had grown to seven thousand in less than six months, but when the Plague revealed itself, the population had been decimated within two weeks. Only a few businesses remained open, including a saloon and a general store which had fewer and fewer goods to sell as the hours passed.

The town's walkways had been laid using timber planks and were bare with no one to walk across. Fanciful signs, moving slightly in the stale air, hung in front of low eves, ready to announce a barber shop, dressmaker, laundry, or butcher to anyone who cared to notice. A large flat board had been posted on the side of the tallest building and stated clearly for all newcomers to read, "Enter At Your Own Risk."

Sophie winced at the sign thinking of the intrepid miners who had continued to venture into the newly discovered mining camps with hopes that they could make their fortunes before the

Plague claimed their lives. Greed had usurped fear and after four years of devastating illness, the West had become synonymous with imminent death.

The young girl reached for the monitor again and squinted to be sure of the mechanism's reading. It was round in shape like a man's pocket watch, and besides tracking the miles she had traveled, was able to detect the smallest amount of Plague infestation by measuring the air's magnetic energy. She wound the mechanism using her thumb to make sure the tiny steel gears were working and waited for the monitor to react. The needle on the dial remained unmoving, giving her confidence that the dreaded disease was no longer active in the town.

Spotting an open doorway, she heard the faint echo of music. She tied her horse to a post and entered the saloon, inquiring about Miles immediately.

A thin old man glanced up from behind a bar counter and answered with no enthusiasm for the subject. "You with the supply wagons?" He quickly noticed she was traveling alone. "He's out back, built himself a place."

"Is there no one else in this town?" Sophie asked, noticing a dark-haired woman dressed in a leather corset and violet satin skirt playing the piano.

The owner looked askance at the visitor and intimated by his sour expression that he didn't want to answer questions. "He's out back," he repeated dryly.

A smile crossed over Sophie's face when she heard confirmation of the man she loved so dearly. The object of obsession which had driven her through the blighted country was a doctor who was her elder by sixteen years. Her angular frame and exquisite features had attracted the older man, and when he spotted her rare beauty he became resolved to have her.

Sophie would never have been quick to succumb to the charms of any man, but Miles Sidlow was no ordinary specimen.

He had the unparalleled benefit of being the most handsome man most women would ever lay their eyes upon. Fair-skinned with dark hair, dark eyes, and a bewitching glare, Miles seemed able to seduce any person he encountered, even the dead. His charms and relentless interest in the spirit world quickly opened doors to wealthy patrons who paid large sums of money to attempt contact with their deceased loved ones. He held séances and card readings and after several successful sessions forecasting the fortunes of his clients and bringing the dead back to life if only through a distant knocking or a cold gust of air, the doctor gained a reputation as a master of the occult.

It was his special talents that inspired his most brilliant idea. In his latest letter to Sophie, he hinted at a new method to capture the images of the departed. The invention would enable the dead to gaze back at the viewer with all the longing of the living. Despite the obvious excitement of the doctor's tone, the letter mentioned no more on the subject except that he had been digging in the abandoned mines and needed more supplies to complete his work.

Sophie circled around the main street toward a newly constructed building with a high roofline. Puffs of white smoke were billowing out of a metal shaft from the rooftop and a low groan of an engine could be heard along with a series of dull pounding noises. She recognized the two mules that belonged to Miles, along with his horse, a dark brown mare, tethered and grazing nearby.

Before she could locate the entrance, the doctor showed himself. He appeared in a leather apron, leather gauntlets, and a pair of oversized protective goggles rimmed in copper resting atop his head. His dark eyes lit up when he saw his paramour and he rushed to wrap his arms around her.

"You're here at last!" he bellowed. "I was hoping to see you last week! Well never mind all that, you have found me in the middle of turning stone into crystalline glass!"

Sophie allowed herself to be held tightly then remembered that she hadn't bathed in several days and the accumulated filth of travel would be apparent. "I must look a sight," she said timidly, pulling at her soiled blouse.

"You look beautiful to me," he gushed. "Come closer my dear, how I have missed you! I am curious, what did the monitor read when you entered town?"

"The dial didn't move," Sophie answered.

"Marvelous, when we return to civilization, I'll have to go straight to manufacture. There is no time to lose!"

Sophie felt familiar dread as the doctor's thoughts turned towards his obsessive interest in science, and held him longer in a vain attempt to hold his attention. After a long embrace, Sophie asked what he had been working on.

"Darling, you can't imagine what wonders I have found. I think I am on the edge of a major breakthrough, a real discovery that could change the course of human understanding!"

"Tell me my love, what have you found?"

"Not now, we have to get you situated first. You must be hungry and, of course, you will be wanting a bath," he insisted. "I'll get one of the girls to help."

Sophie was perplexed. "What girls?"

"When I arrived, most of the town had been evacuated, I told you in my letter?" he reminded. "Well, several of the saloon girls remained behind to help. And now with the aid of the monitors, they feel safe to stay."

Sophie wondered if she should be jealous. "Is it safe to stay?" she asked.

"It is now, but to tell the truth, they remained behind to scavenge. You see my love, most of the town left without taking the time to pack all their belongings and some were so fearful of getting the Plague that they didn't even bother to take their most precious possessions. I've heard bags of gold were hidden in discreet places," Miles said with little interest. "But who could care for a trivial thing like gold? I have on my hands an invention that will be worth millions!"

"Miles, I am concerned about more than the Plague. The Redeemers have been seen about thirty miles from here. I heard someone talking about it at the train station. Are you sure we should stay?" Sophie asked.

As she spoke, she felt a dreadful foreboding. Caravans of survivors roamed the territory led by an exuberant, opportunistic preacher promising salvation for the souls of the departed if the living would offer ritual sacrifices at the gravesites. An odd panoply of wagons and carriages loaded with the grief-stricken made their sojourn from one abandoned town to another. Sophie had not yet encountered the Train of Redemption, or Redeemers as they had become known, and she felt herself lucky. Many of the people on board were fanatical and believed that the Plague was God's plan to purify the world before the foretold second coming.

"No worries my dear, from what I hear the caravan was seen traveling south, far away from Beggars Gulch. And besides I can't leave now, I have found what I need at the mines and I can't be sure that these minerals exist anywhere else!"

Sophie felt apprehensive. "Are you close to being finished?"

"Very close, and tonight I will show you what I've been working on." He concluded with a quick kiss on her lips. "All will be revealed this evening."

Sophie felt the blood rush to her face and the tingle of expectant desire sent a shiver over her skin. All she wanted in that moment was for him to desire her in return. "Tonight then," she replied obediently.

When Sophie returned to the saloon, two women inspected the new arrival and had poised themselves against the bar counter with their elbows resting on the shiny wood. The girl in the violet satin skirt spoke first and asked Sophie how she knew the doctor.

"He's my husband. Well not exactly, but he will be," Sophie replied too quickly.

"You're his girl then?" asked a sultry redheaded woman. She struck an imposing figure wearing leather pants tightly cinched around her waist with a metal studded belt. A large gun was slung low on her curvy hips and a lit a cigarette dangled from her rouged mouth.

"Yes, I am," Sophie answered strongly. "Miles said to ask for accommodations."

The red-haired woman laughed aloud but gave the young girl a friendly look. "You're just a kid," she said moving her green eyes up and down Sophie's thin frame. "I'm Maddie and this is Lou, we'll be glad to help out. Anything for the doc."

The other woman winked and added, "It's really Lucille but I never liked that name. Sounds too ladylike and one thing this town ain't, is a place for ladies."

Sophie smiled slightly and added that she would appreciate a bath.

"Sure thing, Doc got us all set up with hot running water any time we like. What do you think about that?" Maddie asked, leading Sophie up the stairway.

"I will be needing a room as well," Sophie mentioned.

"No problem, Doc's got a special room set up for you two love birds." Maddie grinned.

The large dressing room contained an oversized porcelain tub and a collection of velvet upholstered settees and armchairs. One wall was entirely composed of a complex maze of copper pipes forming a series of curved lines that pumped water into the tub.

"It took a while to figure this thing out, but Doc did a real kindness," Maddie said as she took both hands to turn the oversized wheeled levers which controlled the flow and heat of the water. "When the doc got here, he asked what us girls most wanted in exchange for his keep and we all answered the same thing!"

When the tub was filled, Sophie began to peel off her dirty garments. The red-haired woman had remained in the room, positioning herself on a blue velvet chair to watch the young girl undress. "Don't worry about me none, I like men in that way." Maddie laughed. "Just is a rare occurrence that we get visitors and I feel like talkin' to someone new. Once in a blue moon, we get a wanderer looking for a new home but no one wants to stay for long."

"You must have supply wagons come through," Sophie said. She felt self-conscious removing her blouse, revealing her bare white shoulders to the stranger.

"They must hire the ugliest drivers they can find. I haven't seen one good-lookin' man in months, except for the doc," Maddie said shaking her head in disappointment. "You wouldn't consider sharin' him for a price?" she asked, laughing.

Sophie returned a nervous glare.

"Why is a good lookin' gal like you travelin' all alone?" Maddie asked.

"Miles needs supplies for his work and I help by bringing them."

The redhead grinned and replied, "I guess I'd follow that man anywhere if he asked. You must get tired though, trampin' through the hills carryin' his stuff?"

"I don't mind; his work is important," the young girl answered strongly. "He is on a verge of a major breakthrough with his research."

"I'm sure he is. He keeps busy right enough, always going back and forth to the cemetery," Maddie replied, still grinning.

"How do you mean?"

Maddie propped one leg up over another chair and let out a long exhale filled with smoke. "It ain't safe being alone out there with those fool Redeemers terrorizing everyone. You would think that the end times was at hand the way they carry on. If it wasn't for the gold Lou and I keep managing to find we woulda left this place a long time back. Just when we think we have dug through every hiding place, we find another stash of treasure. But I still say that there's no sense hangin' on when trouble is lurkin'. Lou and I got plans to take off when the next supply wagon comes this way."

"Have you seen them?" Sophie asked, now relaxed and submerged in luxurious steamy warmth. "The Redeemers, I mean."

"I wish I could say that I hadn't. About a month ago, Lou and I took a ride to Bodie. We had heard that there were jobs for girls like us and the rumors were that the Plague hadn't hit so bad. Well come to find out nothing much was left and the Train of Redemption had followed close behind. We barely managed to escape before being taken."

Sophie ran the bar of sweet smelling soap across her shoulders and asked for more details.

"If they take you alive, it ain't pretty. You have to confess and repent or they take matters into their own hands," Maddie replied.

"Confess to what?"

"Doing Devil's work I guess. They got it into their heads that all this Plague business is punishment for people being sinful and that their duty is to purify the souls of the living."

"What were they like?" Sophie asked, thankful she had never encountered the feared caravans.

"What me and Lou saw would make anyone shake in fear. They're crazy people bent on making this place a living hell. Like it isn't already."

"But what did you see?" Sophie asked.

"I'll tell you this, you hear 'em before you see 'em. Drums are banging and what sounds like high-pitched screams puts pains in your ears. They say it's to scare away the demons before they enter a town but I say it's the sound of pure evil coming in."

"I guess we should be thankful that they are far away from us," Sophie said feeling relieved.

"Don't get too cozy," Maddie said with a wry grin. "They got ways of gettin' to places that I've never seen before."

"What do you mean?"

"The leader, some half-man, half-giant, got himself a flying machine. I wouldn't have believed it myself but as we were gettin' the hell outta Bodie, Lou spotted it over the town."

Sophie's eyes grew big and she questioned further into the strange machine.

"He leads his camp of crazies from the air and it's like he's some type of god. The thing looks like a big balloon with steam coming out the back. Just hope you never see it, cause if you do, you're in trouble and that might be the last thing you ever set your pretty eyes on."

The door opened suddenly and Lou walked in. "Doc says to finish up quick, he aching to show you his invention!"

Maddie let out a loud laugh causing her cigarette to tilt downward. "I wish he was aching for me!"

Sophie dressed quickly, rummaging through her bags to find the prettiest dress she had. Maddie helped to lace up her corset and to fasten the white lace dress. A dainty hat decorated with silk roses and ribbons was positioned atop blond curls. As Sophie was pulling on her high heeled boots, Maddie exclaimed, "Pretty as a picture. Too bad the preacher left, you woulda made a fine bride."

Miles was waiting in the saloon when Sophie came down the stairwell. The doctor looked up and smiled widely, remarking how lovely the young girl looked. Holding out his hand, he led her through a back doorway to his alley laboratory.

"You are lovely enough to make a man forget his true calling," Miles said sweetly. "But I am eager to show you what I have been working on." The doctor quickly turned his attention to the shelves and tables which held containers of fluids, minerals, and open journals. Taking up most of the room was a machine constructed of metal hammers and pistons riveted together with steel bolts. It was systematically stamping rocks into powder with large vertical movements while a small steam compression engine powered the process.

"Look darling, this is the key to my success," he said proudly reaching into a pail of rocks located by the machine.

Sophie picked up one of the small stones and held it to the light. They were light in weight and transparent, but held a variety of colors depending on the angle they were held.

"It's the iridescent quality that makes them special," the doctor added picking up a container filled with radiant rock dust. "I have never seen this mineral before. When I was searching through the mine shafts for copper, I saw these stones peeking through the rock and my instincts told me it could be the ingredient I was looking for. After the material has been ground thoroughly, it is heated to a very high degree until it turns to a type of glass. It is amazing how similar its properties are to silica."

"What will you use it for my love?"

"Darling, what if I told you that I have found a way to harness the souls of the dead? Not just for a moment but forever!"

Sophie held a look of alarm.

The doctor picked up a shard of newly made iridescent glass and held it to the light for Sophie to view. "Look here my dear, once I fill a container made with this glass, the soul reveals itself in the most startling manner!"

"What souls are you speaking of?"

"The souls of the dead. That is why I need to be here. To have ready access to the bodies without interference from family members or the authorities."

"But darling, how do you retrieve the souls? Surely they don't just appear and offer themselves to you?"

"How right you are!" the doctor grinned widely. "That is another process. Now come here and I'll explain. Paranormal scientists, such as myself, have always wondered if the physical body holds any part of the soul after death. And after many failed experiments, I was ready to give up on the notion. But when I used bone material, I began to have success. I take the bones and grind it in with these powders. When it is well mixed, sulfurous gas is added. But I have to be very careful at this point for if the mixture is not placed and sealed into the glass immediately, the soul will dissipate into the air and then I have no hope of retrieving it."

"Bone material?" Sophie asked, afraid to further inquire into whose bones he was using.

"Yes my dear, your beloved fiancé has been grave robbing. But there was no other way and I am sure that once the aggrieved see the phenomenal results, there can be no reasonable objection."

Sophie gave the doctor a confused look. "You said you have had success?"

"I have had the greatest success ever imagined! I feel like everything in my life has led me to this place and to this fantastic discovery!"

Miles opened a cloth-lined box and carefully lifted out his new invention. Sophie held it in her hands and felt the lightness of the glass and its contents. The container was round with a narrow neck and resembled a genie bottle. It had been tightly sealed with a rubber-lined metal lid and, at first glance, did not appear to have anything inside.

"I'll bring it closer to the light and you will see for yourself the miracles that modern science has to offer," Miles said with excitement.

The surface of the glass reflected an array of soft pastel colors and Sophie looked deeply into the interior to find what had been promised. To her horror, a human face was looking back.

"Miles, I see someone!"

"Of course darling, that is the point exactly!"

"But who is that?"

"A young girl who was buried last month. I have found the more recent the person has died, the easier it is to access the soul."

Sophie peered once more into the glass and asked Miles to move it closer to the sunlight. The image became clear, revealing the distressed expression of a young girl. Her head and face were readily visible while her body was faded and seemed composed of mist.

"Can she see me?" Sophie asked noticing that the girl's eyes were fixed back at her.

"Yes, I believe she can. Isn't it amazing my dear! For the first time in human history, we have captured the soul!"

"What is her name?" Sophie asked, feeling the ghost's despair.

"I believe it was Vivian. Pretty isn't she?" Miles said seemingly unaware that the spirit inside his contraption could be suffering.

Sophie stared into the spirit's soft blue eyes and wanted to give comfort. "Can she hear me?"

"I think so. All indications are that, after death, the soul continues to have some sensory abilities. Go ahead and say something," he suggested.

"Can you see or hear me Vivian?" Sophie asked sweetly. "Are you happy in there?"

"Darling what a question, really!"

The animated face stared back at Sophie and returned an expression of understanding.

"She can hear me Miles!" Sophie exclaimed.

"How marvelous!" Miles replied. "Oh darling, what a future we are going to have! We will be the hit of New York, London, and Paris! All the world will wonder at my invention!"

Sophie continued to stare into the glass and wondered how the doctor's new invention would be received in a world filled with superstition and fear. "My love, you truly are a genius," she began cautiously, "but have you considered the possibility that the idea of capturing souls may be unpopular?"

"Ridiculous!" the doctor bellowed. "How can you think of such nonsense? Man is a rational creature and when he is introduced to the wonders of science, all the skepticism subsides. History proves that. And besides, we have to have faith in the power of intellect and reason. For without man's higher nature, we are nothing but brute savages!"

"My love, my only concern is that you may not receive the reaction you anticipate."

"I will be declared a national treasure!" Miles said with his chest broadened. "I have no doubt that I will be celebrated and that my invention will be the wonder of the age!"

Sophie looked at her beloved with curiosity regarding his expectations.

"Darling, you must see as I do," the doctor began with a persuasive grin. "We all want to believe that we can be with our loved ones after death. Yes, of course I have been successful at making sporadic contact with the spirit world but what I have just created is a connection that will last forever! No one will ever have to feel that their loss was permanent. How could any rational person object to such a miracle?"

"What will happen to her?" Sophie asked. "Her family can't know of her condition?"

"I plan on releasing Vivian as soon as I have another specimen. As for her family, they left and do not need to know. No harm has been done to dear Vivian. But for now, I have produced just one glass container and it allows for only one soul at a time."

"Where will she go?"

"Into the spirit world I suppose. Perhaps one day, I'll call on her at one of my séances."

The evening was drawing near and the doctor observed that Sophie had been greatly affected and needed time to rest. He arranged for a light supper in the saloon and for a quiet night where he could offer the physical assurances that the young girl longed for. Sophie was grateful for the rest and the affections he generously bestowed and in the intoxicating moment of the lover's embrace, Miles once again promised marriage along with his undying love.

As the five inhabitants of the town slept in quiet darkness, a distant howling grew and permeated through the main street. It was a sound most dwellers of frontier towns had grown accustomed to as coyotes had always densely populated the West, making their nocturnal cries of no importance and no cause for alarm.

The screams were heard first by Maddie and Lou. By the time Sophie and Miles awoke, the drum beats had begun along with the clanging of bells. Miles jumped to his feet and struggled to find the kerosene lamp. Tuning up the flame, he moved the curtains aside and motioned for Sophie to stay away from the windows. "What is that infernal noise? I thought there was no one here except us?"

Sophie shuddered in fear. She knew who was outside and what they had come for. Whispering in a frantic voice, she cried, "Miles, we have to leave now! We can escape through the back, our horses are tied together! Quickly before they find us!"

THE FALL wait

"Darling what are you talking about? Why should we leave?" Miles asked.

Before Sophie could answer, the door opened and Maddie and Lou rushed in. "Get some clothes on!" Maddie yelled, grabbing the white lace dress from the foot of the bed and throwing it at Sophie.

"Is it them?" Sophie asked, her voice trembling. She fell out of bed and slid on the dress, able to only partially fasten the back buttons herself before struggling to pull on her boots.

"It's them all right," Lou answered. "They snuck up to catch us off our guard!"

"Miles, we can still make it out of here," Sophie reminded, barely hearing herself speak over the noise of the Redeemers.

"If you can, make your move! Lou and I will cover from the front of the saloon!" Maddie offered, taking her pistol and swinging a gun belt filled with bullets over her shoulders. "Those crazies aren't gonna take me alive, I can tell you that!"

"Miles we have to go!" Sophie pleaded.

The doctor took another look out the window. "I can't see anyone from here. I'm sure they can be reasoned with. No one in their right mind would hurt innocent strangers and what could we have possibly done to incur their wrath?" Miles replied calmly. "I'll go down and explain that we are merely guests of this establishment and that I am a man of science conducting work for the benefit of mankind. Surely they will be responsive to my explanation."

"They'll be responsive all right!" Maddie yelled back. "They'll beat the devil out of you then burn what's left! Don't be a fool Doc, get out with your girl while you can."

Miles looked at his frightened fiancée in her lovely white dress and smiled. "I have more work to do here. I'm not ready to leave."

Sophie felt her heart pounding and looked to the other girls for support. "What are you saying my love? We have to go!"

"My dear, if I leave now, my work may never be finished," the doctor said with conviction.

"Miles, they will kill us! Don't you understand?"

"Darling, give me a chance to explain myself to the crowd and you'll see that reason always prevails over emotion. As a man of science I owe humanity the chance to prove themselves as rational creatures. Now I'll go down to the street and you stay with Maddie and Lou. I'm sure this misunderstanding will only take a moment to resolve."

Miles buttoned his vest and slipped on his overcoat, then gave one last kiss to his betrothed. "Darling, I love you more than life itself. We will always be together, trust me." And with the dash of a man striving toward a valiant mission, the doctor exited the room to face the mob.

"Sophie can you hear me?" Lou asked, seeing that the young girl was frozen in fear. Giving Sophie a quick, strong shake of the shoulders, she shouted, "Wake up, we have to go!"

"He's gone," Sophie said in a barely audible voice. "He left and he won't be back."

"We have to get outta here!" Maddie said grabbing her by the arm. "Let's go, maybe the doc will make it out, but I know if we stay they'll burn us for sure."

Sophie felt herself pulled out of the room and moved down the stairwell and out the back door to where the horses were.

"Get on, Sophie. We gotta place prepared where we can go 'til this thing blows over," Maddie instructed while hoisting herself onto the saddle behind the young girl.

Lou had mounted the second horse and turned the reins to face the other two riders. "We'll come back to get the gold. Maddie and me hid it real good. No one can find it. I don't care how hard they look!"

As Miles walked out onto the deserted main street, he glanced up and down the road and saw nothing but darkness. The noises had ceased and only the sounds of shutting doors from within the hotel could be heard. The doctor looked for any signs of life and was perplexed to see none. Then in an instant flash of light, the distant darkness was illuminated by ferocious flames. The Redeemers, encamped around the cemetery in full preparation for their night of terror, held hundreds of lit torches.

Miles pulled back from the sudden spectacle. He considered the importance of his research and that if he turned to escape, he may never finish what could be the greatest invention of his life. He rationalized that he could not be held accountable for the advent of the disease or for its disastrous effects and that if he retained his composure and spoke as a man of science, he would be understood. Against his better judgment and the tingling of fear that had begun to vibrate through his body, he proceeded toward the flames.

White-painted faces and charcoal-rimmed eyes stood out against the church's whiteness as they turned to face him. They appeared as corpses animated by the firelight. The women wore formal dresses of fine silk and velvet and the men were attired in waistcoats with colorful cravats. The illusion of morbid elegance was enhanced by the dark red bloodstains which covered their clothes and pieces of bone that hung from their necks in remembrance of past triumphs.

When the full attention of the congregants was upon the doctor, a shrill cry was let out followed by hundreds more creating a deafening noise. Miles placed his hands over his ears, the shrieks penetrating his skull.

Suddenly the crowd was silent, their eyes in tight focus. Miles followed the direction of their collective gaze and looked up in wonderment at the immense shadow descending upon them. The banging of drums and the shrill screams resumed and the supersized airship landed, surprising the doctor who had never witnessed such a strange contraption. The air-filled balloon was larger than the church. Billowing steam blew from the back engine's oversized propellers creating specters of white clouds against the blackness of the night sky. A large, railed platform was suspended below the airship by a series of cables and pulleys revealing a man who seemed to magically appear from a mysterious realm. The crowd continued in hysterical raves as the man stepped out from the machine.

The leader conducted the renewed hysteria for several minutes before restoring command. He proceeded forward in thick boots and a large top hat made of black leather and trimmed in black velvet. His barrel chest was barely contained by a white, ruffled shirt and long coat striped in satin. Amulets of human bones hung in front of his bared white skin. He raised an enormous chalk-colored hand bringing a feather adorned staff high into the air and muttered an incantation in a strange tongue that the doctor did not recognize. Taking a step closer to the captive, he stared into the doctor's eyes and said in a deep growl, "Is your soul prepared?"

Sophie had fled the town not able to turn back. Maddie had kept the horses at a full gallop and only when they were at a safe distance did Sophie realize the horror that had occurred. From the high vantage point in the hills, she could see over the rooftops of the town towards the direction of the cemetery. The ominous glow of the firelight revealed the morbid gathering. The Redeemers had encircled the doctor who was on his knees begging for his life.

"There was nothing we could do Sophie. When they found out he was playing with the souls of the dead, he wouldn't have stood a chance." Maddie said, placing her hand on the girl's shoulder.

Sophie's eyes filled with numb tears as she turned her head away not able to watch the funeral pyre that had been assembled for the man she loved so completely.

"Better to not see," Lou said kindly. "All we can do now is remember him."

The three women remained in hiding for three days while the Redeemers roamed the town looking for survivors. The saloon owner and the manager of the general store were never seen again. The girls supposed the two men had somehow escaped the wrath which had befallen the doctor.

During the long dark nights, hideous cries and sacrilegious prayers could be heard from the town below and the women waited and watched. Only when the insane mob had finished with their incantations, bonfires, and ritualistic blood letting, the madness ceased. The Redeemers finally departed, leaving Beggars Gulch a hollowed out place for the living.

Sophie carefully picked through the burnt ashes of the bonfires looking for any trace of her beloved. Most of the debris was unidentifiable and had been scattered into the barren landscape by the dry winds. She continued her quest until, finally, she located what looked to be a fragment of bone. In a moment of reverence, she picked it up and held it to her heart. A piece of Miles had been found and she knew what she had to do.

The laboratory had not been touched during the terrible reckoning. The doctor's notebooks and equipment were just as he had left them. Sophie donned the protective goggles and gloves and began to gather the ingredients following the doctor's meticulous notes. The container holding Vivian was removed from the box and after saying a final farewell, Sophie lifted the lid and witnessed the vapor dissipate into the heavens above. "Goodbye Vivian, bless you and thank you for everything,"

Sophie said. And in a swift motion, she inserted the ground particles of bone, gas, and mineral powders in its place.

Sophie whispered a special prayer along with her soul's true longing, "I love you and miss you so much." The young girl looked searchingly for the soul of her beloved. She held the glass to the light, fixating on its contents hoping for the connection she desperately needed. Through the prism of watery tears and the gleam of iridescent glass, the handsome face of the man who held her heart appeared. Feeling her grief pull her closer to him, their eyes met and in the mist of bone dust, Sophie saw Miles gazing back at her with the intensity of amorous longing. The doctor smiled a loving smile and Sophie's heart filled with joy knowing that they would never again be parted.

FLIGHT PLANS

J. Lea López

I LIKE THE DISTANCE WHERE YOU can still see the buildings and cars and roads, like little Lego blocks scattered among winding rivers and concrete streams. Where clouds hang by some miracle of physics. Where civilization—or what used to be that—is diminished to a series of grids blocked in brown and green.

Still so much green.

It was easy to forget there were such things as trees when I was neck-deep in life, and career, and happy hour in the city. It's even easier to forget about the verdant parts when you're ankle-deep in the red and black of death. When the only green is putrid decay.

I like the way my head floats up here, like I'm dreaming. It could be a dream, for all I can tell up here. It looks the same as it always has. From this distance, everything always looks still, whether there's bustling life below or not.

I like the rumble of the plane's engine and how it hums beneath my thighs, feet, fingertips. It reminds me that I'm alive. Right now. Up here. Where I can imagine there's still life below in those quiet squares of land. It distracts me from the itch in the back of my throat, in my eyes and nose.

That's how it starts. The end starts with an itch and ends with....

I like the marriage of gold and blue and emerald on the horizon. It's cruel that sunset is still beautiful with no one left to see it.

I like the reading on the fuel gauge. I'll need the fire. Just in case.

The horizon disappears from view and all I see is living earth. I don't know whether it will give birth to anything like the human race again, or if it will simply swallow our remnants in a cocoon of green and brown and blue.

I like the sound of the world without the engine. Silence. Not too long ago the air was heavy with anguished cries, first from the initial victims of the virus, then the loved ones who had to watch them suffer, and finally from those same survivors as they eventually succumbed to the illness themselves. After that it was the daily symphony of gunshots. On every street, in every state, one by one. Mercy killings and suicide pacts.

It only took a few hundred years, and the spread of one deadly virus, for the United States to finally come together in a moment of true social and political unity. When the government issued guns to every citizen regardless of race, color, or creed, relieved all law enforcement and military of duty, and ceased all commerce activities, there was no uproar about gun control or border safety or prosperity. It was far too late to worry about that.

I didn't think I would, but I like the electric sensation of free-fall. Eternally into the landscape below. Mother Earth my last companion.

She beckons.

So many shades. Jade. Turquoise. Emerald. My birthstone, not that it means anything now. I memorize each hue as they draw near, that I might take the memory with me. The virus will not claim me.

I like that memories don't flash before me. No faces of family, friends, or lovers flooding in to obscure my view of green.

I like the pull of gravity.

Close enough to see the forest for the trees. A cacophony of green.

Close enough to see leaves. Close enough....

In the end, I like that death is so green.

THE LAST SACRIFICE

Judy Croome

DEATH STALKS I, RAX-UL-CAN, through the jungle with eyes as cold and yellow as those of the silky black *yaguara*, cat of the night.

I, Rax-ul-can, beloved of the gods, bringer of rain and abundant harvests, Lord of the Four Elements and mighty High Priest of the great city Quchichualxe, welcome death.

Unlike so many others, I do not fear death.

Why should I?

There will be no journey to Zitaltá, the underworld of fire, for me. The gods I have served so well since I was a boy not ten *quin* old will reward me in death as well as they did in life.

Did I not begin with death? My mother died even as I wailed my first cry. Having sacrificed herself to give me life she, too, avoided the fire journey. And, from the incomparable gifts I showed from a young age, she clearly interceded with the gods and our ancestors, who rained their blessings on me from the moment of my creation.

My father, even as he mourned my mother, knew I was destined for greatness.

"Rax, you will have treasures piled higher than the tallest ceiba tree," he would say. "You will be powerful beyond measure. You will have thousands worship at your feet."

"Will I, *Daat*?" I knew he spoke the truth, for I felt the power of the gods within me, but I liked to hear him tell the dream story of my birth night.

"Z'uz'umatz told me so," my father would say, his warm bronze skin weathered by the many seasons he had spent in this world. His voice would deepen with faith and innocence, for he had no doubt the magnificent god Z'uz'umatz himself had spoken as he lay sleeping.

"How did you know it was Z'uz'umatz?"

"By the soaring feathered plumes on his head and the scales on his body; by the red-and-blue feathers on his arms and the forked tongue flickering between the countless teeth in his beak."

"What did he say?"

His hand, calloused from the hours he spent elaborately carving the history of our people into the stone stela, for he was not of noble birth and nor was I, touched my face and he would whisper, "He would tell me that you, Rax-ul-can, will be his greatest *Thizan Qai*. No other High Priest will equal you in skill. No other High Priest will bring as much honor to the gods as you."

So it came to be.

When, at the end of my ninth summer, I entered the walls of the Temple of Cholchun for the first time, I soon became the most favored of all the apprentice *thizans*.

By the time I was fifteen *quin*, my reputation as Skywatcher, and as a superbly accurate thrower of the seeds, had outgrown even my renowned skill at healing the most obscure illnesses.

Kings who were enemies came to our people as supplicants.

"We seek the wisdom of Rax-ul-can," their emissaries would say, as they spread in front of me an untold wealth in *yaguara* pelts, brightly colored forest birds, mounds of corn, and heaps of gold and gems.

I would heal their sons and read their destinies with an easy skill way beyond my youth.

"*Xa i'ik teech atsul.*" They would wish me good luck as they left and, truly, the gods blessed me with the greatest of good fortunes.

Just as Z'uz'umatz had promised my father.

They would also leave behind the daughters of their kings and nobles: to marry or to sacrifice as I saw fit. Only the most beautiful of the maidens paraded in front of me and, on the same day I became *Thizan Qai*, High Priest of the Temple of Cholchun in the great city Quchichualxe, I married my first wife. She was a good woman, for she gave me many fine sons. And Eme-chal.

Aaah. Eme-chal.

If her mother—teeth sharpened and charmingly filled with precious hematite, pyrite, and turquoise—was beautiful, my daughter was a goddess. Her long black hair, her unblemished bronze skin and that most generous gift from the gods: her mother did not have to hang beads over her cradle, for Eme-chal was born with both eyes naturally crossed, a source of loveliness and wonder to all who gazed upon her throughout her life.

On the days of the great festivals, Eme-chal would sit on the sleep chamber floor in my many-roomed stone house, near the center of the Royal Court—very different from the simple straw-and-mud *cah* I lived in with my father before I became High Priest. Eyes wide with wonder, she would watch her mother prepare me for my duties.

First, there was the scrape of the sharpened obsidian over my skin, cleansing away the remnants of my human sweat and stains. Then would come the fat of the wild pig, scented with jasmine and warmed gently over a fire, before being rubbed over my naked body until it glistened and gleamed like the stars of the sky-gods. The same oil would be combed through my hair, making it shine blacker than the pelt of the *yaguara* as my wife twisted it into a knot tight enough to hold the headdress of a High Priest as exalted as I.

Next, she would wrap the three woven cloths around my loins, the last intricate fold covering my *ph'ok*, my virility, in a soft drape to my knees; then she slipped my feet into sandals made of vine, twisted with threads of fine-beaten gold.

Finally, my primary wife garbed me in the signs of my high office: the long red cloak, the golden collar studded with jewels, and the elaborate headdress, with its lofty macaw feathers of yellow, green, and blue, which would tremble vigorously with even the smallest movement I made.

"Come, daughter," I'd call Eme-chal. Unafraid of my imposing height, and the azure blue tattoos embellishing my face and arms, she'd uncurl herself to run to me with the grace of a deer. Laughing at her eagerness, I'd lift her onto the high wooden table and she would help me slip the golden bracelets with their jangling ornaments onto my wrists. I watched her watch the glittering rewards of my magnificent priesthood: she'd run her chubby fingers over the metal, enraptured by the soft buttery feel.

Her mouth, as tender as the bud of the passion flower, pursed with awe, as I bent my head with deliberate stateliness, making the feathers dance and sway until they tickled her ears and she'd giggle, exclaiming, "*Daat!*"

"*Thizan Qai!*" her mother would correct her. "When he is so dressed, he is not your *Daat*. He is Rax-ul-can, High Priest of the great city Quchichualxe, and all the forests that surround it."

She'd only giggle harder, her baby hands doing their best to capture the swooping feathers of my headdress.

"Your mother is correct," I would say as sternly as I could.

She'd ignore us both and stand high on her toes, reaching up to trace the whirling blue tattoos that adorned my face, before snuggling her head into my shoulder, her tiny hand clutching my arm.

"*Daat*," she'd say, and no admonishment could change her mind.

She kept that possessive grip on me as we walked beyond the streets of our great city and up to the entrance of the soaring pyramid that was the Temple of Cholchun. The tips of her plump fingers played with the bones and feathers dangling from my golden armlets, as if feeling them made her more connected to me as we trudged past the roaring waters of the Sacred Falls, above which I now sit on the temple wall and wait for death. The jungle fell silent as we passed, as if all its wild creatures knew the power of I who walked by.

When we reached the top of the colossal steps leading up to the temple doors, the phalanx of men waiting smiled at the sight we made: the small, beautiful girl-child clinging so lovingly to the arm of her father, their most imposing High Priest.

But even Eme-chal knew she was forbidden to go beyond those massive stone doors the Council of Elders guarded so zealously. No matter how much she implored, no matter what other favors she coaxed from me, she knew I would not take her further than the three-hundred-and-sixty-fifth step.

For beyond that door, carved by her own grandfather, emblazoned with intricate images of the first creation of our people, and framed by two towering stela tapered into bowls in which incense always burned, was the inner shrine where I performed the most sacred, the most holy, of my duties.

For what she did not know, what she could not know, was that beyond that door was where I lifted high the Blade of Faith and offered the bloody hearts of the most beautiful, the most noble souls to one voracious god or another.

The roar of a solitary *yaguara* echoed as it leapt out of silence onto an unsuspecting tapir. The jungle that grew thick and lush around the Sacred Falls pressed down on me, and I gasped for my next breath as thousands of voices called to me from the depths of the dark jade waters of the pools beneath the Falls. The voices of the gods called too, whispering that it was not enough, however many souls I'd already sacrificed, it would never be enough to prevent the apocalypse that approached.

My recent visions were stronger with each night that passed.

Eme-chal, my beautiful Eme-chal, had taken to appearing in my dreams as a young child. Her dream eyes filled with mysteries and love, even as her dream mouth poured forth the future's shadowy secrets.

"Canoes, long canoes, bigger even than some of our temples," she said, "are coming to our land from the great ocean flowing under the rising sun."

She told of what she saw in the far off place where she now lived. "Men—no, not men—gods, twice taller even than you, *Daat*, when you are dressed for the great festivals. White woven cloths tied above their canoes capture the breath of the gods, driving them to our shores. Their faces, half covered in thick black hair, are as bronzed as ours. But beneath their strange silver breast plates, their bodies glow whiter than the light of the moon goddess as she rides the full moon through the dark heavens."

In my dreams, and when I woke remembering her words, I shook my head in disbelief. Such pre-eminent men could surely not exist?

"These strange peoples bring death," Eme-chal whispered the next night, and the next.

"I do not fear death," I said.

"They bring destruction," she moaned.

"Destruction is already upon us," I said, thinking that it was when she was a child but fourteen *quin*, her loveliness already overshadowing the soft beauty of the sacred frangipani, that the gods had begun to desert me.

She had no memory of that year, nor the death and destruction that followed as I offered the gods more and more blood sacrifices to appease the anger that had so suddenly overtaken them. For surely they were angry beyond compare when they no longer granted me what I most longed for?

"Just one more sacrifice, *Daat*," my dream Eme-chal sighed. "Just one last sacrifice." Her languorous hands reached out, baby fingers curling as they had once curled around my armlets as we walked up the stairs to the temple. "All your doubts will be gone, swallowed up as the mist of the morning swallows up the great Temple of Cholchun. All your fears, too, will melt as the mist melts when Ah Q'uatchil wakes his sun chariot and, once more, you will know only the love of the gods, not their anger."

At first, I ignored her dream voice; such a sacrifice—a single soul—would not appease the gods' displeasure when all the sacrifices I had made in the last ten *quin* had not satisfied them.

Not even the Festival of Blood had satisfied them. They had not heard my pleas then, nor granted my request. Could one sacrifice do what all the others had not?

The Festival of Blood.

The thought of it still burned through my veins until I could no longer sit in the contemplative pose I'd held for more hours than I could remember, here at the Sacred Falls next to the Temple of Cholchun, my sanctuary for almost a lifetime. Uncrossing my legs, I stood without needing aid from the dozen *thizans* who waited silently for my commands. The younger neophytes, not yet schooled in masking their reactions, showed veneration at my feat. I was secretly proud that, even at my age, my movements had barely set the feathers in my headdress quivering.

I stood as tall and sturdy as the old ceiba tree I'd planted to thank the gods the day Eme-chal was born. When the blood tingled to life in my feet again, I stepped over the old straw doll that I'd woven for her—her favorite toy until the day she went from virgin daughter to noble woman.

She'd never been more beautiful than when I led her to her destiny.

I'd never forgotten that day. The holy marriage of Rax-ul-can's only daughter was a day to celebrate before the entire city.

The sun god Ah Q'uatchil shone his pleasure on us, adding radiance to the excitement, the eagerness, lighting Eme-chal from within. Trust and faith, in both her father and her gods, to guide her true, added a divine glow to her golden skin.

That day ten summers ago I, too, shared both her trust and faith, for then I was still the gods' favored one: I was Rax-ul-can, beloved of the gods, bringer of rain and abundant harvests, Lord of the Four Elements and mighty High Priest of the great city Quchichualxe, obedient servant and faithful believer.

And yet I have been empty of both faith and trust since that day I gave my Eme-chal away.

What father wants to give his beloved daughter to another, never to see her again?

Nothing the gods gifted me with after that day could fill the void left by Eme-chal's absence.

No sacrifice I made to the gods helped me.

Not even the Festival of Blood stopped the stuttering of my heart, as it yearned for my daughter, virgin no longer but now a wedded bride.

* * *

"Twenty thousand virgins," I said to the Lord Warrior, when he asked what I thought would appease the gods' anger in the fifth season of poor harvest after Eme-chal had left.

"With respect, *Thizan Qai*," he bowed low, his fingers curling tightly around his bow to stop their shaking as he feared my displeasure. "How can you sacrifice *twenty thousand* maidens in four days?"

"Per day," I corrected him, holding my face as impassive as the stones in the temple when he blanched. I'd not forgotten how he'd laughed and staggered around, drunk with delight and honeyed *b'ocolatl*, the day I said goodbye to Eme-chal. I threw a challenging look around the Council of Elders, the leaping flames of the fire they circled highlighting their aged faces, more deeply lined with worry as they debated a way to end the poor harvests that continued to bring our faltering nation to the edge of starvation.

"Eighty thousand virgins in total? That's impossible! The Lord Warrior could never capture so many before the Festival of the Sleeping Sun," said the eldest of the council members.

"Nothing is impossible," I said, "when it's done on the command of the gods."

I met his eyes then, careful to keep all the emptiness in my soul well hidden. He, too, had taken too much pleasure at the sight of Eme-chal in her wedding finery. "Is that not what you told me once? Before Eme-chal's holy marriage?"

His gaze dropped first and, with a curt laugh, I kicked sand into the fire, killing the light, as I reiterated my command to Yum Xipe, Lord Warrior of the nation's armies.

"I have read the signs in the skies. You have three moons to bring the necessary sacrifices. None older than fourteen *quin*. All must have pure blood, or the gods will remain unforgiving."

What a fool I was!

Why did I still believe that the gods cared about us? They had long forsaken us. Even I, Rax-ul-can, most preferred of their priests, was no longer favored.

Within three moons, I had my eighty thousand maidens. As the moon goddess drew a cloak across the face of the sun god and brought night at midday we started the sacrifices.

For four days, the halls of the temple rang with the sound of dozens of blades, slicing and cutting. Rivers of blood flowed down the temple steps, turning the waters of the Sacred Falls from jade to red as every council member, every nobleman, even the youngest *thizan*, made sacrifice after sacrifice until Festival of the Sleeping Sun became known as the Festival of Blood.

The stench of death filled our city for weeks.

But the greatest stench came from inside me, for it was only then, as I waited and waited amongst the decaying piles of young girls, that I finally knew my gods had betrayed me.

I had not lost my faith when I could no longer bring the rains. I had not lost my trust when I could no longer bring victory after victory to our warriors.

I had not even stopped believing in the gods' favor ten summers ago when I walked Eme-chal up the stairs and, for the first time in her young life, allowed her to pass through the great stone door into the inner shrine of the Temple of Cholchun, where I performed my most holy duty as High Priest.

I still believed in their promises even as, in the smoky half-light I stripped her bare and spread-eagled her on the stone altar, binding her arms and her legs with vines her mother had woven. I daubed her with *azul*, the sticky mix of clay and indigo añil shining wetly on her naked limbs as the straw torches burned as feverishly as the lascivious eyes of her waiting bridegrooms, the fierce faces of the gods painted on the ceiling and the walls.

As I smoothed the last stroke of paint around the gate of her purity, the *thizans* carried the bowl of precious honeyed *b'ocolatl* to Eme-chal. She drank her fill then I, and the waiting Council of Elders, emptied the bowl. Soon the flames became faces and the humming in our heads became visions. We began the sacred bloodletting, calling the ancestors' spirits, praising the gods with howls of rapture as the bone spikes lacerated our bodies.

It was my duty as Rax-ul-can, father no longer but the most High Priest of the Temple of Cholchun, savior of our peoples, to forever bind my Eme-chal in sacred union with the gods themselves.

I danced closer and closer to the sacrificial altar, chanting the age-old vows, blood running from my ears, my tongue, and my nipples. With a scream of agony, I pierced my *ph'ok* and, with one thrust, filled her with all the virile power the gods had endowed me. The blood of her maidenhood sprang forth, uniting with the blood of the gods pouring forth from my *ph'ok*. The consecration of this holy union had begun.

My Eme-chal did me proud that day of her marriage to the gods of our people.

She flinched, but not once did she cry out; not even as the Council of Elders—as was expected by virtue of their worldly representation of the gods—took their turn clambering up the altar to mix their bleeding *ph'oks* with Eme-chal's fragile soul. She lay there, accepting her sacred destiny with all the nobility of her young heart. She showed no fear. Her eyes, dazed from the honeyed *b'ocolatl*, were wide with trust and love, and clung to mine all through the ordeal of this sacred marriage ceremony as her multitude of priestly husbands, each representing one of our gods, took his turn at that torn and bloodied gate.

When the youngest *thizan*, younger even than she, had finished, she lay still, believing in the gods, believing in *me*, because I had told her this sacrifice, this marriage to the gods of her body and of her soul, was what the gods needed to save us all.

I gave her a small nod of approval and as I stepped up to the altar and laid my hand on her tender thigh, bloodied with the mix of blood and priestly power, my brave girl allowed the first flicker of pain and relief to creep into her beautiful eyes.

It was then I felt the first of my doubts that would ultimately consume me, yet I dipped my hand between her thighs to scoop up the holy fluid and, around her budding breasts, drew a circle on her chest, a circle that marked the site of her living heart. I kept my hand there, feeling the slow thud, and waited for the gods to show me their favor.

When they remained still and silent, I knew they were not yet satisfied.

I raised high the Blade of Faith. The flames of the torches lighting the cavernous hall glimmered wickedly over its obsidian sheen and, as we had just joined her body with that of the gods, I prepared to join her soul with theirs to save our people.

The chants from around the altar changed pitch, reaching a crescendo and, with my faith guiding me—or blinding me—I struck straight and true, the blade sinking so deep into Emechal's bone and flesh, the shock reverberated up my arm, rattling the bones and feathers she had so liked to cling to.

With my skill and the strength developed after so many years as High Priest, I worked quickly. The fading light of trust still shone in her eyes even as I held her wildly beating heart high above my headdress and sang my prayers to the gods who watched over us.

The *thizans*, squealing with excitement, sliced through the plaited vines holding her to the altar. They carried her to the very edge of the wall of sacrifice, beneath which all the people of our great city, drunk on the common *calbhé* and their hope, waited along with the gods, her Divine Husbands, and threw her body and heart over the Sacred Falls into the pools far below.

As the purifying waters embraced her with thundering haste—or perhaps that was the hungry gods welcoming her—I couldn't help but throw a triumphant glance at the Council of Elders, as if to say, "You're right. Nothing is impossible!"

For when they first came to me, complaining that my rituals no longer worked and my predictions were inaccurate, that the gods had removed us from their favor, I had laughed at them and said, "Never. All the gods need is the right sacrifice. I will find the most beautiful, the most pure bride alive and the gods will return to shower us with their gifts."

"Eme-chal," someone had called. "Eme-chal is the one the gods want."

"Impossible!" I'd shouted, leaping to my feet and waving my fist in the direction of the faceless voice. "Eme-chal is my daughter! My only daughter! To sacrifice her would be impossible!"

"For you, Rax-ul-can," the calm voices of the Council continued, "For you, a High Priest so honored by the gods that the great god Z'uz'umatz himself appeared at your birth, nothing is impossible."

So it came to be.

Throughout the week of fasting leading to Eme-chal's wedding day I believed nothing was impossible. I believed, too, that the gods would stay my hand with some magnificent sign from the heavens. Even as I held high the Blade of Faith, I trusted that they would somehow bring my Eme-chal back to me, her body whole and pure again, her face alight with love.

From the day I watched Eme-chal's heart slowly stop beating in my hand, I had searched and searched for the one gift that would show the gods how worthy I was. For I believed that, if I gave them what they desired, if they wanted to honor me beyond imagination, they could give me one small gift in return: my Eme-chal.

With every sacrifice, with every *quin* that passed, my faith dimmed, for still the gods did not return her. It was two summers ago that I realized the gods needed more, much more, than they had ever received before.

When I read the sky charts and saw the coming of the Sleeping Sun, I knew that such an auspicious heavenly event would be the perfect time to hold a festival so enormous, sacrifices so unprecedented, that the selfish gods would send my Eme-chal back at last. Surely, I believed, even for the angriest of gods, eighty thousand brides would be enough of an exchange for one small daughter?

But, as the days after what became known as the Festival of Blood passed, and the thousands of bodies rotted on the stairs of the temple and in the waters of the Falls, all but the last remnants of my faith rotted and decayed too.

Until Eme-chal, with her dream murmurs of the annihilation awaiting my people in the near time, came to me in my dreams and spoke to me of the last sacrifice.

I shook myself from my trance and moved to the very edge of the Sacred Falls, next to the low wall over which I had seen so many noble sacrifices plunge. My headdress quivered and the youngest *thizan*—my grandson, eldest son of my eldest son—laughed with delight. He knew how those feathers could tickle.

Because he reminded me so much of Eme-chal, I smiled at him.

"Come," I said, calling him over in a voice softened by memories of my daughter. My eldest son made a sound of protest, quickly silenced with a look. I called my grandson again. "Come, boy, you shall honor the gods and your ancestors by helping me. Bring the honeyed *b'ocolatl* and let us drink."

His small face alight with pride and effort, he hurried to stand next to me, his head barely extending above the wall of sacrifice and I began the preparatory ritual I had done so often.

I drank from the painted bowl to take my mind into the vision world; I pierced my nose and my ears, so I could more clearly hear the voices of the gods as they guided the Blade of Faith. Finally, I pierced my *ph'ok*.

My holy blood ran free and fast. With my left hand, the one Eme-chal had loved to hold so tightly, I dipped into the pool of my blood and drew a perfect circle on my chest. With my right hand, I lifted the Blade of Faith as high as I could. I gave the *thizans* the signal and their chants echoed through my head as I shouted the words of my final offering and slammed the obsidian blade deep into my chest.

With the gods' strength keeping me upright and the voice of my daughter urging me on as she called from the dark, dark pools below, I finished the slice and cut. For the good of my people, I tore out my still beating heart, offering the last sacrifice to my gods.

Only then did I surrender and let myself tumble over the low temple wall into the icy waters of the Sacred Falls. A terrible dimness overtook me and, at last, I joined my Eme-chal where she waited, forever embraced in the arms of the gods whom I had loved and served so well.

Acknowledgements

The Elephant's Bookshelf Press anthologies have been a lot of fun to produce, but they have also required a fair amount of work added onto already busy lives. As if that weren't enough, the theme of the apocalypse challenged us to make sure the stories didn't all sound the same. One can't only have zombies running amok, after all.

I want to thank my partners, Mindy McGinnis and Cat Woods, who helped coordinate the anthology and who were never afraid to voice a contrary opinion. In the same breath, I must applaud Jean Oram, our chief copy editor, who stepped in as though she'd been part of the team from the get-go. She also submitted a wonderful story that shows love and longing will survive the apocalypse. (Cat Woods copy edited Jean's story.)

Once again, our captivating cover was designed by Calista Taylor (Covers by Cali www.coversbycali.com), and R.C. Lewis served again as book designer, a challenging task made more difficult in this age of multiple presentation methods.

On a personal note, I want to acknowledge the assistance of Mary Serbe—artist, educator, and friend—who along with Mindy and Cat read early versions of my story. They all offered valuable insight that improved it greatly. And R.S. Mellette shared his background in the theater arts to help us with the formatting of Mindy's story.

Our first anthology helped build some word of mouth among a myriad of writing groups including AgentQuery Connect, which I consider the most helpful, honest, and supportive online writing community. For *Spring Fevers*, we approached writers we knew, but *The Fall* attracted submissions from writers near and far, including many whose work I'd never read before. I have new appreciation for how hard it can be for literary agents who sift through piles of queries on a daily basis. I can only imagine what *Summer Burn*, the next anthology, will bring. I'm looking forward to it, and hope you are as well.

ABOUT THE AUTHORS

P.S. Carrillo

P.S. Carrillo is an attorney and writer of fiction. Her published works include the YA novel, *Desert Passage* (Arte Publico Press 2008) and the short story, "No One Remembers," in the award winning collection of YA mystery, *You Don't Have A Clue* (Arte Publico Press 2011). Patricia's interests in psychology, history and mythology inform her writing. She resides in California with her chihuahua, Sammijo, and her website is www.pscarrillo.com.

Judy Croome

Judy Croome lives and writes in Johannesburg, South Africa. Shortlisted in the African Writing Flash Fiction 2011 competition, Judy's short stories and poems have appeared in various magazines and anthologies, both local and international. Her books "a Lamp at Midday" (2012) and "Dancing in the Shadows of Love" (2011) are available on Amazon. Judy loves her family, cats, exploring the meaning of life, chocolate, cats, rainy days, ancient churches with their ancient graveyards, cats, meditation and solitude. Oh, and cats. Judy loves cats (who already appear to have discovered the meaning of life.) Visit Judy on her blog www.judycroome.blogspot.com or join her on Twitter @judy_croome.

Ryan Graudin

When she's not writing and drifting around the globe, Ryan Graudin enjoys hunting through thrift stores and scouting out perfect apocalypse hideouts in her native Charleston, SC. Her novel *All That Glows*, the story of a Faery who falls in love with the prince she's forced to guard, is due out with HarperTeen in 2013. You can learn about all of these things and more at ryangraudin.blogspot.com. You can also follow her on Twitter at @ryangraudin.

R.C. Lewis

R.C. Lewis teaches math to teenagers by day and writes geeky-chic young adult novels every spare moment she gets. Her debut novel, *Stitching Snow*, will be published by Disney-Hyperion in summer 2014. When she isn't busy grading quizzes, she blogs at crossingthehelix.blogspot.com and www.fromthewriteangle.com, and you can find her on Twitter @RC_Lewis.

J. Lea Lopez

J. Lea Lopez writes upmarket women's fiction and erotica and has had short fiction published with *Oysters & Chocolate* and *Divine Dirt Quarterly*. She loves Dean Koontz, Jell-O, cute animal pictures, and bad sci-fi movies. She dislikes mean people, bad sex scenes, and writing bios about herself in third-person. For musings on the writing life and more, check out her blog at jlealopez.blogspot.com or on Twitter @JLeaLopez, where she spends way too much of her time.

Mindy McGinnis

Mindy McGinnis is a YA author and librarian. Her debut, *Not a Drop to Drink*, will be coming from Katherine Tegen / Harper Collins in the fall of 2013. Mindy runs a blog for aspiring writers at Writer, Writer, Pants on Fire and contributes to the group blogs From the Write Angle, The Lucky 13s, Friday the Thirteeners, Book Pregnant, and The Class of 2k13. Mindy also serves as a moderator for the writing community at AgentQuery Connect under the screen name bigblackcat97 and tweets from @bigblackcat97. For another story by Mindy, download *Spring Fevers*.

R.S. Mellette

R.S. Mellette, originally from Winston-Salem, N.C., now lives in Sherman Oaks, California, where he slaves away at turning his imaginary friends into real people. While working on *Xena: Warrior Princess*, he created and wrote The Xena Scrolls for Universal's New Media department. When an episode aired based on his characters, it became the first intellectual property to move from the Internet to television. R.S. works and blogs for the film festival Dances With Films (www.danceswithfilms.com) and also blogs at www.fromthewriteangle.com.

Alexandra Tys O'Connor

Alexandra Tys (rhymes with ice) writes exclusively for the young adult market. Her writing has a basis in the equally fascinating and terrifying world of psychology where human nature and experience collide. When she's not plotting her next psychological thriller, Alexandra is neck-deep in other people's divorces. As an advocate for children, she helps parents navigate the treacherous waters of parenting time and child custody. She invites you to peek inside her blog, Whispering Minds (alexandratysoconnor.blogspot.com), where anything is possible and not everything is as it seems.

Jean Oram

Jean Oram will read pretty much anything, but her true love lies with humorous chick lit (some call it women's fiction). This is her first short story other than that 1.5-pager she cowrote with a friend back in grade 9 English which, oddly enough, was not quite apocalyptic and not at all chick lit. She plans to release her first chick lit eBook, "Champagne and Lemon Drops," in November 2012. When Jean isn't ripping up the slopes on her skis, camping, traveling, hanging out with her kids, coaching soccer, or drinking tea, you can usually find her geeking out online on one of her websites. She shares play activities for kids at www.itsallkidsplay.ca and writing tips and some other (future) goofy stuff at www.jeanoram.com. You can also find her on Twitter @JeanOram.

Matt Sinclair

Matt Sinclair is a New York City-based journalist covering philanthropy and charity, primarily in the United States—a field he has covered since the mid-1990s. He also has worked extensively as a freelance writer, covering a wide range of topics including arts and culture, sports (primarily baseball), business, education, health care, parenting, politics, and, of course, writing. He is a site moderator at AgentQuery Connect and blogs at elephantsbookshelf.blogspot.com and www.fromthewriteangle.com. In 2012, he established Elephant's Bookshelf Press, LLC, publisher of *Spring Fevers* and *The Fall* and aims to launch the website of Elephant's Bookshelf Press (www.elephantsbookshelfpress.com) by the end of October 2012 so long as his twin 3-year-olds don't consume his brains before then.

A.M. Supinger

A.M. Supinger is a 24-year-old Floridian living in South Dakota. She writes when not working, and spends the rest of her spare time buried under piles of books. Her husband, two schnauzers, and two cats all bark and claw their way into her most precious moments. Her stories in *Spring Fevers* represented her first foray into print, but she has a blog full of free stories at innerowlet.blogspot.com, and she tweets @AMSupinger.

Amy Trueblood

Amy Trueblood is a freelance writer who spends most of her time penning press releases for her favorite nonprofit. When not "chasing the crazy" dream of being published, you can find her rereading her favorite YA books, running, or slurping down her favorite mango iced tea. For interesting musings on writing, in-depth author interviews, and agents' perspectives on those "first five pages" of a manuscript, check out her blog www.chasingthecrazies.wordpress.com or follow her on Twitter @atrueblood5.

Cat Woods

Found on the windy ridge between South Dakota and Minnesota, Cat Woods collects novel fodder like window blinds collect dust bunnies. When she's not raising her four kids, two hunting labs and one dear hubby, Cat pens stories for readers of all ages. She's a juvenile lit junkie, Scrabble addict and moderator on AgentQuery Connect. Her whimsical writing journey can be found on Words from the Woods (www.catwoods.wordpress.com), while her writing wisdom appears at www.fromthewriteangle.com.

COMING JUNE 2013

SUMMER BURN

NOT ALL RELATIONSHIPS ARE MEANT TO LAST.

Made in the USA
Coppell, TX
13 October 2023

22817367R00113